VILLAGE OF TEARS

VILLAGE OF TEARS

CHRISTOPHER ABBOTT

Order this book online at www.trafford.com
or email orders@trafford.com

Most Trafford titles are also available at major online book retailers.

Printed in the United States of America.

ISBN: 978-1-4120-6103-2 (sc)
ISBN: 978-1-4251-9539-7 (e)

Trafford rev. 02/04/2014

 www.trafford.com
North America & international
toll-free: 1 888 232 4444 (USA & Canada)
fax: 812 355 4082

PROLOGUE

E VEN THOUGH HE WAS on the verge of freedom, he could not stop longing for the place that only two months before he had risked his life to escape from. Wet, cold, and so tired, he remembered the familiar songs of relief he often sang after a blistering day spent in the fields, and the words echoed in his mind, even now somehow finding their way to his blue lips and chattering teeth. Of course there was punishment, at the end of a whip mostly. But even that now seemed like a small price to pay for sneaking out after dark to meet pretty girls under the lazy, sheltering willows.

Promises made by others had brought him here, so far away from his family and home. They told him fantastic, glorious stories about the idea of freedom for which he now suffered with only rags on his feet to protect them from the snow. They had said that if he ran away and found them, they would show him how to get to the safe place without getting caught and whipped, or worse yet, hobbled. So one night, he kissed his mother on the head and told her he was going to get some water. But when he stepped outside the one room shack, the only home he had ever known, he ran through the night, thinking he could fly.

He did not leave just because he could make his own way. He had always wanted to see the world and be like the man in the drawing he had once seen in the master's house, standing on a ship and looking out across endless water. Someday, he knew, he would go back to his mother, but only after he had sailed around the world and brought its treasure back with him.

For eight weeks, he and five others like him had walked and crawled along the countryside under cover of night. Several times, after they slept in the shadows during the day, they woke up to find a different guide who always told them the same thing; to be quiet and as still as they could so that no person could find them. They were given only stale bread to eat, but sometimes they would snatch fruit from the trees and pumpkins from the fields to fill their screaming stomachs.

Although no one ever told him where they were, he knew they were finally close to safety when the air became sharp and cold, letting loose the frozen white powder that tasted sweet on his lips. When it first fell on them, they laughed silently and danced with each other arm in arm. But when it became deep, and their feet grew numb, they cursed the cold with each exhausting step.

Near the end, the old man walking next to him grunted and sat down in the snow. He closed his eyes and shook his head each time someone reached out a hand to help him up. He pointed to his feet. They were hard and frozen, dead and bloody. When the guide tried to warm them between his hands, the old man moaned and fell back. A few minutes later he took his last breath. They buried him in the snow among some trees where he would not be discovered until the spring.

Sometimes they slept outside, other times they were led through back doors to small, dusty rooms or fruit cellars where they were forced to sleep on top of each other. But it mattered little, for at the end of each long night of traveling they were too exhausted to care about confined quarters or their own stench.

On the fifty-sixth day, they were told by a pale woman with blonde hair and crooked teeth that they would only have to stay in one more cellar, and that the next day they would be taken to a farm where they could work for money and sleep in a warm barn. When night fell she led them through a thick, haunted forest and along frozen fences to a house that looked like the one where his master lived. The pale woman led them downstairs into a dark room and told them to sit on some straw in the corner of the room. When the time was right, she said, someone would bring them out and the owner of the house would give them food and clothes.

Minutes, however, turned into silent hours and still he waited. He tried to imagine what he would do there, what his job would be. He did not think that anything could grow in the gray cold, and he wondered if he could care for the animals, or perhaps wait on the family and stay out of the rain. He thought about money he would earn and he hoped it would be enough to buy him passage to the nearest port, maybe in New York. He heard there were others like him there who lived and worked on ships like the one in the picture.

His stomach grumbled and he remembered that he had not had anything to eat in almost two days. In an attempt to distract himself from the hunger pains, he leaned back on the soggy straw and curled up, trying to stay warm. He could feel something sharp against his back and reached behind him to find that a rusty nail was the source of his discomfort. He was glad for the discovery though, because it would give him something to do while he waited.

He rolled over onto his stomach and crawled until he found the clammy, flaking wall. There were many words he wanted to put there, but he only knew how to write the name his mother gave him. He scratched and carved until his fingers were cramped and numb. Finally, he blew away the dust to reveal the name that he knew would one day be the stuff of stories told to children.

Franklin Carver.

Satisfied with his creation, and having forgotten his hunger for the moment, he drifted off into a light sleep filled with images of tall ships and women in white flowing gowns who smiled and gracefully bowed to one another. Suddenly, he was trapped in snow, shivering and clawing at the wall of white around him. He wanted the pretty ladies to cover him with their dresses and keep him warm. He panicked and screamed, not knowing if he was dreaming or if the world itself had collapsed around him. He sat up and rubbed his sleep-swollen eyes.

A tall, silent figure in a long jacket blocked the open doorway. His thin silhouette stood out dramatically against a cold, moonlit sky. His head turned slowly to one side and he nodded, acknowledging some unseen presence outside. Although he was wearing a hat with a wide brim which otherwise hid his face, Franklin could make out sharp features in profile against the burning winter moon.

The man slowly turned back and surveyed the human contents of the room as if waiting for a volunteer. Sensing this, Franklin raised a trembling hand. He had decided that he would show his willingness to please his employer; perhaps he would even have the opportunity to choose the best of the quarters in the barn.

"All right, you first. The rest of you get in line; I'll take you one at a time."

Although he was starving, and his legs were cramped from hours of inactivity, he jumped to his feet. The thin man motioned with a gloved hand for him to follow and they climbed the few stairs to the grounds beyond. As they walked silently, Franklin noticed that two other figures fell in line behind them. They continued across a yard and down a dirt lane. In the distance, he could see a gray and white barn illuminated by two lanterns that hung on either side of a doorway.

Franklin wanted to say that he would be a good worker, that he would always be respectful in every duty he was given, but he decided that it was not yet his place to speak until he had greeted his employer. As they neared the barn, he imagined a warm bed of dry straw and the comforting snorts of resting horses lulling him into a deep sleep. But they passed the friendly glow of the lanterns and walked past the barn toward the haunted, black forest.

Franklin's heart sank as he realized that he would probably be pushed into some old broken down shed with holes in the roof and frozen mud for a floor. Nevertheless, he told himself that he must not complain because any wage is better than no wage, especially when it would gain him passage to the sea.

They walked silently through the light snow that covered the path, which gradually narrowed and became more impassable. Franklin's feet grew numb and he began to stumble. He knew that he could not walk much farther, and he prayed for the sight of any rickety shelter if it would mean an end to his journey.

They stopped at the base of a towering oak tree that seemed to stand guard over a snow covered clearing beyond. Before Franklin could even catch his breath and wonder why they had halted when no shelter was in sight, the thin man turned and swung something hard and heavy against his skull.

The inky blackness gave way to bright flashes of pain firing across his disoriented mind like lightning. As he awoke, and sensation returned, he dreamed that a dog was chewing on the side of his head, its drool cascading down his cheek. He jerked instinctively to avoid the imagined demon tearing at his flesh, but memory followed the pain and he realized he had been injured by the very people who were to protect and nurture him.

He tried to crawl through the snow, but the pain paralyzed him. He cried and tried to scream for his sweet mother he had kissed and lied to so long ago, but the sound amounted to nothing more than a gurgle through his swollen and shattered face.

"He's still alive!" a voice yelled from just above him.

"Well, here's the knife," another voice in the distance casually responded. "Finish it and bury him."

In spite of his crushed skull, Franklin could feel the cold blade brush across his throat and he knew that death was near. As his blood poured onto the thirsty earth, he thought of the oceans he would never gaze across or conquer, and he wondered if anyone would ever know how he came to meet his maker.

Chapter 1

IT WAS NOT THE warm morning sun or the heavy traffic moving ceaselessly on street below that woke Caleb. Rather, he was prodded from much needed sleep by the sheer will of his dog, Sara. She stared at him intensely from his bedside and wagged her tail in anticipation of a foray into the world outside. As he stirred in response to her primordial power, she took this as her cue to assist him to full consciousness. She licked his face furiously.

When her tongue threatened to suffocate him, he reached over, gently pushed her head away, and pulled the covers over his face. But Sara was familiar with this routine, and she jumped on the bed and began pulling at the sheets as if she were digging a hole in the dirt. Caleb sat up, rubbing his neck where Sara's nails had left a welt, and swung his feet onto the floor.

While he waited for his balance to be restored, he rubbed his eyes and watched Sara pace happily back and forth in front of him with a slimy piece of rawhide in her mouth that she had obviously been chewing on while he slept. Sara was a Viszla, bred for endurance and speed on the plains of Hungary. This heritage was revealed in her deep chest, long, slender legs and rippling muscles, which became visible under her short chestnut coat as she moved. Caleb imagined her running in a wide-open place, gracefully hurdling any obstacles while she pursued the scent of unseen things, and he was sad that in her one year of life she had been confined only to the city of Philadelphia and the length of a dirty nylon leash. He thought that it was cruel to deny her mastery of her elements and vowed that he would one day walk off into the forest with her and disappear without a trace.

Caleb stood slowly, patted Sara on the head and shuffled across the hardwood floor, painfully aware that he was hung over and that he might easily slip on the smooth surface in his disoriented condition, as he had done before.

He found the bathroom and fumbled for the light switch in the dark. The florescent light streamed through the slits of his eyes and shocked his weary senses. He raised his heavy head to meet his own reflection in the mirror and noticed that his eyes were glassy and bloodshot, obscuring their usual green intensity, and evidencing the consumption of alcohol and cigarettes the night before.

Caleb stepped back from the mirror and flexed his well muscled torso in an adolescent display, attempting to reassure himself that by running and performing calisthenics in his apartment before he went to work each morning he was able to adequately maintain his 30 year old body against the ravages of his more destructive habits.

Caleb stepped outside his apartment that Saturday morning with Sara straining at the leash. The warm sun rejuvenated his body and cleared his foggy mind. Sara too seemed more content on such a beautiful spring day. As they moved together down the tree-lined sidewalk, she often stopped and pawed at some scent emanating from the concrete. Her body quivered with excitement each time she captured a strange smell and her tail wagged back and forth with such force that her hindquarters swung to and fro in unison.

When Sara stopped to investigate a rusting fire hydrant, Caleb surveyed his neighborhood, noting its attributes in an attempt to assure himself that he had done well for himself and all was right with the world.

On either side of the street, the red brick apartment buildings with painted black trim rose up only to the height of the massive oaks shading the sidewalks. This was no doubt intended to give residents a cozy feeling akin to that which one experienced living in a small town. Yet, the entrance to each of the buildings was adorned with a green awning with gold stripes, suggesting that anyone who passed underneath was wealthy, civilized and cosmopolitan.

It was certainly a strange combination of design elements, but it nevertheless created a feeling of pride and satisfaction in those who chose to live here. He could not help thinking, though, that this observation was true only if you could ignore the fact that the electric city constantly pulsated around you, making it the center of your life.

Caleb tugged on the leash and they jogged across the street while dodging the weekend traffic. They continued running down the block to a small park. The clearing occupied about an acre and was mostly grass except where a paved path ran across it diagonally. In the center was a concrete bench where old people who lived nearby often sat wrapped in wool sweaters even on the hottest of days.

Although it was only an island of green in a sea of hard stone, it was enough to ease his anxiety when he came here and took off his shoes to let the blades of grass tickle his feet.

On that morning, Caleb had the place to himself. He was tempted to let Sara run off the leash for a few moments, but he quickly decided against it because he knew that if she darted toward the busy street he would not be able to match her speed. Instead, he jogged in circles around the grass so Sara could stretch her legs. After five laps he was drenched in sweat reeking of alcohol and greasy food.

As they circled to complete a sixth lap, Caleb noticed a group of adolescents who had entered the park from the opposite side. Judging from their size and stature, he guessed they were all between eleven and thirteen years old. They had formed a circle and were waving their

arms and cheering about something in the center of their group that
Caleb could not see. When he got closer to the gathering, he found a
clear view through a gap between a fat boy wearing patched jeans and
a tall drink of water wearing a white T-shirt and grass-stained khakis. In
the center was a small boy with a crew cut and heavy glasses strapped
to his head with a black sports band. He was being shoved and called
"scrawny shit" by a well-muscled kid wearing a cut-off blue sweatshirt
and a faded Giants baseball hat. The fat boy started shaking his fist and
screaming for a fight.

Somehow sensing his presence, the small boy turned his head and
stared at Caleb through his coke bottle glasses. He could see fear in the
boy's wild blue eyes, grotesquely magnified by the lenses. With quivering
lips the child formed the shape of words meant for Caleb.

Help me please.

The silent plea triggered an explosion in Caleb's mind and hurled him
into the black hole of a memory he had so long ago locked away in his
subconscious.

***

When Caleb was eleven and the world was a glorious place where
he ran barefoot in the summer and dreamed of adventure far from the
shiny suburban neighborhood where he lived, he collided head-on with
a juggernaut. His name was Marcus Pullman, but he was affectionately
known as "Mucus." He was a barrel-chested thirteen year old with long
unkempt red hair and a crooked nose. He was a bully who regularly
terrorized his peers on the block by shoving them to the ground and
twisting their spindly arms until they cried and ran home.

One humid August afternoon, Caleb was returning home after swimming at an abandoned stone quarry when he found Mucus pummeling
one of his playmates, whose name he had long forgotten, with rotten
apples that had fallen into the street from an overgrown tree. Mucus
had backed the whimpering boy into a corner of his open garage and
was throwing the small apples with such force that they disintegrated

when they struck the boy, causing him to howl and beg for mercy with tearful pleas.

Caleb had, until that point, somehow managed to avoid any conflict with Mucus, but he always knew that they would eventually clash when the opportunity was right, and the idea had given him nightmares. Perhaps it was the fear that made him strike.

Caleb glanced down to a pile of fly-covered dog shit rotting and stinking in the heat. He scooped up the soft putrid mass, disrupting the insect banquet. He circled around in front of Mucus, who was cocking his arm to hurl another piece of fruit, and shoved the crap into his face, being sure to fill his gaping mouth with the stuff.

"Leave him alone you asshole!" Caleb screamed at the top of his lungs.

Mucus offered no words in kind, but doubled over and immediately vomited, revealing an unidentifiable meal whose bright yellow color provided a stark contrast to the black excrement. To add insult to injury, Caleb pushed the back of Mucus' sweating head down so he landed face first in the ugly puddle. Then he ran and laughed and felt free and strong. He balanced himself on the curb sometimes as he went, fascinated by his coordination. He would be home in time for dinner, and despite what he had done, he was hungry.

After washing his hands at a spigot on the side of the house, Caleb threw open the back door and walked into the kitchen, where he found his quiet mother as he usually did, busying herself with steaming pots and food in a flurry of activity. She was kind and patient, the other side of his father, who was brash and proud and always stressed from his job as a manager of a chain of auto parts stores.

In fact, that evening his father was busy at work and was not yet home to slug his martinis and curse the neighbors whose lawn, in his opinion, was always overgrown. He was not the type of man to hug his only child, and Caleb grew up with the feeling that his father had given in to his mother's wishes to bear a child only because it was expected by others in the white, picket-fenced world where he struggled so hard to keep pace with every other family on the block.

While they waited for his father, Caleb set the dining room table and then went up to his room with the intention of paging through one of his many worn and faded comic books. He had not yet reached the second floor when he heard the hollow sound of his father's Chevrolet Impala as it pulled into the garage below.

Although he wanted to hop down the stairs and pull on his father's sleeve, he knew to gauge his temper before he approached him. Caleb sat on the top step and listened for the tone of his voice as he came into the kitchen and complained yet again that he was sick and tired of the traffic. Caleb knew that if he tried to gain his attention now he would only prove to be a distraction that his father would casually wave away with a stroke of his hand as if he were a buzzing mosquito. He would wait until his father ate and drank before he told of his victory that day.

As Caleb scrubbed his hands with soap and water in preparation for the meal, he imagined his father nodding and smiling with pride when he learned what Caleb had done to the evil Mucus. He thought his father might bend over and laugh and rub his head in playful frenzy, satisfied that his son would become a man who would quash injustice in all its forms. Maybe he would even be a superhero, and he could hardly wait to get back to his room so he could shut the door and look through his comic books to find an appropriate costume. Caleb was drying his hands on a tattered pink hand towel his mother had given him to spare what she called her "guest towels," despite the fact they never had any guests, when he heard his father yell up the stairs.

"Get down here Caleb...now!" He screamed as if Caleb had broken every window in the house and was hiding now to avoid punishment.

Caleb tried to remember what he might have done to displease his father, but he was sure that no matter what it was, his good deed would surround him like a knight's armor, ready to deflect his father's wrath.

When he got to the bottom of the stairs his father was waiting. He was standing with his hands on his hips. Rolled up shirtsleeves revealed strong, hairy forearms. His head was lowered as if he were concentrating to quell an anger Caleb thought might otherwise result in a terrible scream that would level the house. He remembered noticing for the first time a bald spot on the top of his father's head illuminated by the florescent kitchen lights on the ceiling above him.

But Caleb was not deterred. Like one of his heroes, he stood his ground, and thrust his chest out and dared the rage.

His father looked up with steel blue eyes set deeply in his stubbly face. His square chin barely moved as he spoke through clenched teeth.

"There's a boy standing outside who says you threw dog crap in his face, is that true?"

"Yeah, but..."

"But nothing," he interrupted, not interested in any explanation because he most certainly was embarrassed that anyone in the neighborhood might think he had not raised his child correctly.

"He's waiting outside, and looking for a little payback. I can't say I blame him. If someone threw shit in my face, I would make things right."

"Dad, he's a bully, he always picks on kids."

"So what, then you fight him man to man, you don't pull this sissy stuff and jump him when he's not looking. Now, you get out there and fight like a man."

Caleb stared at his mother, hoping she would throw her apron to floor and gather him up in her arms, so he was safe and warm in her womb, oblivious to the world outside. But his father had followed his wide-eyed gaze and spoke before she could even draw a breath in opposition to the proposed rite of passage.

"Don't even think about getting involved, Lou," he warned as he held out one of his arms to block her anticipated approach. "If the boy doesn't learn to be a man and stand up for his actions now, he'll always be a baby."

Before Caleb could pray to the god who required him to dress up in an ill-fitting corduroy suit every Sunday, his father grabbed him by the arm and dragged him across the kitchen floor. He could see Mucus there beyond the safety of his home, his distorted face pressed against the screen door. He stood back and smiled while Caleb's father swung the door open.

"Sink or swim boy," his father casually quipped, suggesting that this were simply one of the many lessons learned during childhood that Caleb would look back upon with affection. But as Caleb stood face to face with the demon, he knew he would always hate his father and that he would never forget the fear that seemed to be suffocating him.

As Caleb raised his shaking fists up in a posture he had seen in a boxing advertisement somewhere, he suddenly realized how big Mucus was, even for a thirteen year old. He stood at least a head taller than Caleb and probably outweighed him by thirty pounds. Although some of that mass rested uselessly in roll that protruded from his puke-stained T-shirt, his barrel chest and broad shoulders suggested the physical strength Mucus had at his command.

"I'll even let you throw the first punch," he snarled from behind his freckled face as he brushed away a lock of strawberry hair that had fallen over his eyes.

Caleb did not wait for another word. He swung as hard as could, instinctively aiming for the crooked nose. But Mucus was experienced in such matters, and he stepped back quickly. Caleb lost his balance when his blow fell short and he stumbled forward, landing on his knees. He looked up to see Mucus form a grapefruit sized fist with his pudgy fingers. He tried to raise a hand to protect his face, but Mucus slapped it away with his other hand and struck him on the jaw at the corner of his mouth. For an instant, everything was white, then he was looking at the sky and his angry father was standing over him.

"Get up and defend yourself," his father demanded while he grabbed him by his arms and hauled him back up to his feet.

Caleb pushed him away and reached up to his swollen mouth. He could feel the jagged tear in his lip and the blood pouring down the front of his shirt from the wound. He could also taste the sandy grit from a broken tooth. He cried and screamed to his father for help, but he just folded his arms and shook his head with disgust for a son who obviously shamed him.

"You don't get off that easy," Mucus taunted as Caleb turned slowly to face him again. "C'mon, come at me."

This time Caleb ran. He imagined himself bounding over fences and slipping through tiny gaps between buildings. He thought he might run until he did not know where he was, then he would keep on going until he found the ocean. He would forget his house and his parents and his comic books. He would swim and fish and sleep under a palm tree while he pretended he was the only person in the world.

Caleb sprinted across the yard but was caught from behind by Mucus after only a few steps. He never imagined that someone with the consistency of Jell-O could move so quickly. Caleb screamed again and tried to squirm away, but Mucus spun him around and punched him in the center of his chest. With a faint gasp, Caleb fell, unable to talk or scream or even breathe. Mucus dropped to his knees next to him and punched him two more times in the face. As consciousness faded, Caleb could feel Mucus kicking him in the side. The last thing he remembered before the blackness enveloped him was his mother running toward him in what seemed to be slow motion. He cursed her too.

***

Sara rarely barked, and it was the strange sound of her throaty bay that brought Caleb out of the trance. When he realized that the crowd of boys was staring at him and that he had their undivided attention, he told them to go home or he would find out where they lived and call their parents. Although this was an idle threat Caleb often heard from others who happened upon some of his childhood antics, it was nevertheless still effective, albeit to a lesser degree, on a new generation of troublemakers, and the kids grudgingly made their way out of the park.

The little boy with thick glasses smiled at him and ran past in the opposite direction.

CHAPTER 2

WHEN THEY RETURNED TO the dark apartment, Caleb poured some dry dog food for Sara and she ate while he opened the blinds to the sun. Caleb watched as dust particles drifted in and out of the rays of light, becoming visible for a brief moment then disappearing into the shadows. He waved his hand through the air and watched the tiny pieces swirl in the wake.

He took off his wet T-shirt and collapsed on a red velvet couch he'd bought from a balding old woman through a personal ad in the newspaper. Although he had the couch for over a year, whenever he sat down on the cushions with any force they still released the scent of lavender and old wool from somewhere deep inside. The smell was comforting and he could not help but imagine the intimate moments of a quiet life that had unfolded there.

As he basked in the warm light he thought of that day outside his house with Mucus and the pain that was now fresh in his mind. He and his father talked little after that, only exchanging polite words necessary to maintain the facade of decency. But the hatred he had for his father destroyed even that tacit understanding when Caleb was arrested several times as teenager for starting fights and dropped off at home in a police car.

The rift between them also destroyed his parents' marriage. When Caleb was in college his mother called him late one night to say that she had packed her bags and moved in with her sister in California. She said she loved him but she was never coming home again.

His father died a year later of a heart attack, when Caleb was a senior. Because he had retired, no one was even aware of his absence. Noticing a stench and an overflowing mailbox, one of the neighbors his father had tried so hard to impress climbed into the house through an open window and found the rotting corpse some two weeks after the event. On the day of his funeral it was raining and Caleb watched the black ritual from his car while he drank coffee mixed with cream and whiskey.

Then his life twisted and turned at dizzying speed like some malfunctioning roller coaster raging out of control, sure to jump the tracks at the next sharp turn. After barely graduating from college, he took a job tending bar at a blue-collar watering hole in Philadelphia and was consumed by the night world. He worked and drank and talked to toothless would-be heroes who succumbed to evil ex-wives and child support payments.

Many times, Caleb collapsed on his bed as the sun rose and woke up barely in time to see it set beneath the crooked skyline. The wrinkled bills that filled his tip jar were spent gambling on horses and basketball games. He lost it all though, and people came looking for payment of money he only pretended he had.

One morning while he slept quietly and dreamed of a still pond shimmering in the moonlight, he felt rough hands cover his mouth and pin his arms to the bed. He opened his eyes while he was in that netherworld between consciousness and oblivion and saw the evil Mucus staring down at him and smiling. Caleb struggled against his restraints, determined to smite him and claw at his eyes and blame him for his life. But when his wide eyes focused on his assailant, he saw only the blank, impersonal stare of a man hired to do a job. When the thug and his fellow enforcers were finished with Caleb, he was sprawled naked on the floor, tangled in blood-stained sheets and struggling to breath against three broken ribs he was later told had punctured one of his lungs. The thug had said that this was Caleb's only warning, and that if they had to come back another time, they would kill him and cut off his head.

As Caleb lay there burning with pain from his injuries, he thought he saw his old comic book superheroes standing over him. With their hands on their hips, they thrust out their muscular costumed chests and bellowed with hearty laughter as if mocking the weakness and fear his father had instilled in him so many years ago.

Determined not to be a fool in front of his childhood companions again, Caleb slowly raised himself from the floor only to find that the ghosts had withdrawn back to the recesses of his foggy mind. To this day, he was convinced that if his mind had not tricked him in this manner, he would have died there on the dirty floor and joined his father in hell.

But the blows seemed to have jarred loose a burning desire to prove himself. He promptly paid his debt. And although he had no real interest in the law, Caleb decided that law school was the path to redemption and glory. For himself and the imaginary old friends who saved him, he listened to animated professors and studied and did very well, graduating near the top of his class. When he was handed his diploma, he knew his heroes were smiling down on him and he smiled back, savoring the victory. Even his dissatisfaction with work could not rob him of that achievement.

Caleb exhaled slowly and felt the tension flow out on his breath. He leaned back and swung his legs up onto the couch. Sara followed him and curled up at his feet. He closed his eyes and pushed his face into the soft, smooth fabric. He drifted off into sleep and the swirling storm in his mind took the shape of strange things more vivid than any dream should be.

Caleb was on an old ship. Its billowing white sails had captured a warm wind that pushed it through a sea stretching uninterrupted to the horizon.

He walked to the bow and leaned over to see white foam churning and spraying as the ship parted the waves. He looked back over his shoulder, expecting to glimpse the weathered faces of a crew busy tending to the sails and miles of rope that controlled them, but the deck was eerily silent. His shadow disappeared and the sky grew dark while the wind blew down from above with a new-found intensity.

Caleb ran the length of the creaking ship until he found a hatch that was ajar and he climbed down into the blackness. As he descended, smooth rungs of an unseen ladder became rough and varied in size. He realized he was now among the uneven branches of a towering oak tree. He hung down from the lowest limb and dropped a few feet to the ground below. It was covered with leaves, except where patches of bright green moss had found their way to sun.

"Do you know this place?"

The voice seemed familiar and Caleb spun toward the direction of its source. A slender woman with long brown hair and dark pools for eyes was sitting on a rope swing hanging from the limb he had just jumped off. She was wearing a faded sundress worn so thin he could make out the outline of her breasts and dark nipples. Her hair was drawn back in a tight braid revealing her soft, smooth face.

"This is just a tree," he remarked, "no different than any other, and I have seen many such trees."

"Well," she said as she slid off the swing and reached out to caress the rough trunk, "do you recognize anything different about this particular tree?"

"No, not really, except that it is large and so tall that I can't see the top."

"That's right," she acknowledged with a sensual smile. "This tree is so tall and beautiful because it has been nourished with human blood."

"Whose blood?"

"If you find me before you go, I promise that I will tell you. Then you will not be so confused."

Caleb moved toward her, longing to rub his fingers across her hard nipples, but she was not there any longer. Then he felt her warm breath on the back of his neck and he closed his eyes. Without turning, he reached back under her dress and felt the creamy soft skin of her inner thigh. He raised his hand up until he could feel coarse pubic hairs tickle the top of his thumb.

"I know you're afraid," she whispered, "but you have to turn and kiss me so that you will know what I know."

When he looked on her face he shuddered. There were no bright eyes and succulent lips begging for him to take her; only a flat veil of skin devoid of any hint of human features.

"What happened to your face?" he cried and drew back against the tree. "You have no face!"

When Caleb woke up, the sun was beginning to set in the distance, casting the twilight through his window. He sat up and reached over and patted Sara on the head. She had been waiting for him to stir and she jumped up and shook her body, throwing off some invisible substance. Perhaps, he thought, she had been dreaming too. Maybe she envisioned that she was swimming in a glistening pond or rubbing herself in cool dirt and now tried to rid herself of the excess because she could not differentiate between her unconscious actions and reality.

Caleb took a cold shower and dressed casually in jeans and a black polo shirt buttoned to the top. He snatched a blue windbreaker off the back of a chair and made his way out into the city.

Caleb walked the eight blocks over to Market Street, one of the busiest thoroughfares in the city. Young professional couples from the suburbs hurried across intersections to make their reservations at some of the trendiest restaurants on the east coast. After that, they would no doubt move on to exclusive clubs just a few more blocks away and party well into the early morning hours.

But Caleb walked past the tables on the street where people wore their sunglasses after dark, talked on cell phones and perused menus all offering portobella mushrooms in one form or another.

He ducked under a faded green awning that read *Shiny's Pub* and pushed his weight against the heavy oak door he knew always stuck a little, swollen by the humidity. The smoke and darkness enveloped him, welcoming him to the warm anonymity that could only be found in a place where people drank alone at the bar and read newspapers, not sure if it was day or night for the lack of any windows.

"Mr. Magellan," the gray haired bartender smiled, glancing up while he washed glasses in the sink.

"Harry." Caleb smiled back, finding the rickety stool at the far end of the bar as he always did.

"Are you having dinner again, Mr. Magellan?" Harry asked as he made his way toward Caleb, wiping his hands on a towel he always had draped over his shoulder.

"Yeah, let me have the half-pound cheeseburger again, with steak fries. I'll have a pint of Guiness too, Harry."

"You got it," Harry acknowledged with a curt salute, then spun around and shuffled into the kitchen out of sight.

Caleb shook his head. Harry was always there, day or night. He could not ever recall a time he had been there over the past two years that he was not greeted by Harry's sincere smile. He was limping slightly tonight, which made Caleb feel sorry for him, and convinced him that no man in his seventies should have to work so hard.

Caleb glanced around the room. A man, probably in his fifties, wearing a suit, was sipping a martini and staring intently at the newscast on the small television mounted just above him on the wall. At one of the few tables on the floor behind him, a young black couple giggled to one another while they poured beer from a pitcher and gingerly handled slices of steaming pizza.

"Here's your Guiness. Your food will be a couple more minutes. I had to warm up the grill first."

"No problem. Thanks, Harry."

Harry returned to washing glasses in the sink, occasionally holding them up to one of the small lamps suspended from the ceiling to be sure they were clean.

Caleb took several large gulps of the thick black liquid, relishing the cold that slid down his throat and awakened his senses. When he rested the glass back down on the bar, Harry had arrived with a green paper placemat, silverware and his piping hot dinner.

When he was finished eating, Caleb ordered another pint of Guiness and drank it quickly. The alcohol rushed through him, easing his tension and making the world seem distant and puny. The buzz made him feel for a moment as if he were not so lonely, as if the constant shuffle of paperwork that marked his daily routine as a patent attorney was exciting, the stuff of every child's dream about what it would be like to be grown up. At one time, when he was young, he was sure that he would become something great, that he would rule the world. He had trouble accepting that he had crested the wave of his destiny.

Since the beginning of time, millions upon millions of people had come and gone, their lives and minds and personalities lost forever because anyone who ever knew them was already long ago turned to fertilizer. This was no doubt to be Caleb's fate as well. But for Caleb, he would be forgotten even more quickly because he had no family to follow him and he had achieved no milestones that might otherwise secure him a place in collective memory. He had no cure for a disease, no profound ideas for revolutionizing society. He had found no soul mate nor had he formed lifelong friendships. He was simply sitting in a bar at the moment, each second becoming a memory that only he would ever care to recall.

Caleb sighed and shook his head. He reached back into the dusty nooks of his brain. He closed his eyes and squeezed, but he could not find that optimism that he once knew. He could not remember what it was that he once thought might make him worthy of at least a footnote in a boring history book. He did his best to convince himself that his life was everything he hoped it would be. If he were to dwell on his insignificance he would only drink himself to oblivion, as he used to do quite often. Still, some oily bubble of discontent stirred in his breast. So he ordered one more drink to be sure to finally silence the tiny voice that begged him to walk away from it all.

As always, the haze of cigar and cigarette smoke seemed to become a black curtain behind which Caleb found security and warm, albeit fleeting, numbness. But that night would be different because a long-forgotten face found him in the fog.

"Cal Magellan."

Caleb looked up. It had been so long since anyone called him Cal, as if that were a young man he once knew, who had disappeared and had become a face on a torn, faded poster in the back room of a post office somewhere.

The moon-shaped face with small blue eyes was contorted quizzically, highlighting a double chin. A hand was outstretched, but Caleb could only muster a glance while his mind thumbed through its index of identities searching for a match.

"Frazier McCoy here, remember?"

A flood of images filled Caleb's mind. He remembered the awkward, pear-shaped Frazier playing video games on his laptop computer during class in law school while everybody else furiously scribbled notes. When the professor called on Frazier, he would recite some meaningless legalese that would draw a collective snicker from the rest of the students.

Oftentimes he told jokes at parties at the expense of some ethnic group, which inevitably offended almost everybody within earshot. Very quickly Frazier became an outcast. If it were not for the fact that he came from old money, which bought him some measure of dignity, he would have amounted to nothing more than a convenience store clerk. But Caleb suspected that Frazier's purposeful ugliness was a reaction to the fact that he was fat, awkward and unloved. And because he knew that Frazier probably cried in the dark and struggled every day to keep from killing himself, Caleb had befriended him when no one else would even hold the door for him.

"Holy shit...Frazier McCoy."

"In the flesh. I bet you thought you'd never see me again."

Caleb had been virtually certain that he would, in fact, never see his face again after school. Perhaps this was wishful thinking, as Caleb was not quite sure he ever wanted to see him again. Yet, he ached for some conversation, and thought a trip down memory lane might ground him and ease his throbbing anxiety. He was also curious to hear what had become of this strange, lumbering man.

"What the hell are you doing here, Frazier? If you didn't live around here, you would never even know about this place."

"I met some friends down the street for dinner. I saw you come in here when I got out of my car, before we started eating. I just found my way back here when I was done."

Caleb studied him for a moment. He was wearing a suit that naturally followed along his narrow shoulders yet seemed to flow down over his wide stomach and hips without bunching or creasing at any point. His wingtip shoes glistened with a spit shine that was almost as spectacular as the glare from a gold Rolex tightly squeezing his pudgy wrist.

"You look good, Frazier. That must have been some meal." Caleb finally reached out to shake his hand. "Take a seat."

Frazier pulled out a handkerchief and wiped the seat of the stool next to Caleb, then settled his weight on it. He glanced around, then turned to Caleb and leaned an elbow on the bar. He cleared his throat before he spoke, as if he was biding time to prepare what he would say.

"Wait," Caleb interrupted his concentration. "What do want to drink?"

"I'll have a Stoli on the rocks."

Caleb motioned to catch Harry's attention, but he was already pouring the drink.

"Well," Frazier began while he finished the vodka in a single gulp, "after school I went to work for my dad in his import business. It's contracts and such mostly, either somebody doesn't pay or doesn't deliver."

Harry filled Frazier's glass again as soon as it hit the bar. He smiled at Frazier, but Frazier refused to make eye contact.

"What do you import?" Caleb asked.

"You name it, we bring it in. Mostly we buy vodka from Eastern Europe and sell it for three times the price here. It's a good business."

"Where are you living?"

"Right now, I'm in New York, but that may change. My father wants me to move into our house in northern New Jersey, where I grew up. He wants to go to Atlanta to open up a new office and he won't sell the place. He insists that it be kept in the family. I've been telling him to go fuck himself. He wants me up there tonight to meet him because he's leaving for a conference in Atlanta in the morning."

Frazier chuckled, as if pleased with himself that he had stood his ground against his father's edict, and then glanced around to be sure no one was listening.

"I even told him I would turn him into the Feds for some of his practices." The last word he spoke while he used his fingers to simulate quotation marks.

"What do you mean?" Caleb asked, not so dumbfounded by the fact that a child would threaten his father with criminal prosecution as he was by the fact that he admitted to it.

"Forget it, that's not even the point anyway."

Frazier was obviously disgusted with his father. His voice shook with anger as he spoke of him. Caleb sensed that Frazier wanted an emotional punching bag on which to vent his frustration, but Caleb was not as prepared to console him as he had once been. Rather than chance such a one-sided encounter, Caleb remained silent and concentrated on the foam that remained at the bottom of his glass. Caleb suddenly remembered with particular clarity why he had been relieved when they parted ways. He had grown weary of Frazier and even now Caleb lacked the inclination and energy to rescue him from drowning in his own misery. Perhaps this was because Caleb had matured and come to realize that another person's happiness could never be his responsibility. But perhaps it was something else; maybe he was just not as kind as he used to be.

After a moment, Frazier turned to him and feigned a smile.

"What about you, what are you doing?"

"Intellectual property, patents. I work downtown here in a firm."

"Sounds interesting," Frazier muttered sarcastically under his breath, clearly bored with the conversation now that he was no longer the subject of attention. He glanced over to the television and sighed.

"Are you married or anything?" He asked while he stared at the flickering screen.

"No, it's just me and my dog. How about you?"

Frazier turned back and shot him a razor sharp glare.

"What the fuck, am I supposed to be?"

Caleb raised his hands to ward off the verbal assault.

"Hey look Frazier, I'm just making conversation. If you have a problem with it you can walk right back out the door."

Frazier nervously ran a hand through his thinning hair several times in rapid succession, as if the action might somehow release the tension that now seemed to boil up to the top of his head.

"Look, I'm just tired. I've been working some crazy hours."

Caleb only nodded to acknowledge the apology while Harry filled his glass once more.

"This crap between me and my father," Frazier continued, leaning close, "it's making me nuts. Believe me, it's hard to work with family."

Caleb exhaled slowly, letting his anxiety flow out on his breath and dissipate into the air.

"Yeah, I can understand that," he conceded. "It sounds like you need some time away or something."

Frazier rested a hand on Caleb's shoulder.

"That gives me a great idea," he whispered with the mischievous smile of a boy about to pull the wings off of a fly. "How about you stay at our place in New Jersey for a couple of weeks, a house sitter if you will? That will give me some more time to work on my father in Atlanta and beg him to let me stay in New York."

"When, you mean starting tomorrow?"

"Monday's fine. I'm not leaving for Atlanta until tomorrow night."

"I don't know Frazier, that's pretty short notice. I mean, I'm supposed to be back at work on Monday. I'll have to reschedule a lot of things. I haven't had a vacation in a while, but..."

"Do you like the green forest?" Frazier interrupted. "Cool shadows?"

Caleb was intrigued and he was quiet while Frazier spoke. Frazier said it was a paradise; three hundred acres of lush, dark forest, some of which had not been visited by humans since the ancient Indians drank from the clear streams that carved through the valleys. It was a quiet place, he said, where a man could think about anything that happened across his mind at any time of day or night. Frazier said that on some nights, when the moon was shining, you could make out the resident herd of deer bounding through the trees as gracefully as if they could fly.

"When you are finished playing, you can relax in the Jacuzzi in the main house, or take a dip in the lake. Or you can sit on the porch, sip scotch and watch the sun set over the hills."

Frazier exhaled and leaned his back against the bar, obviously proud of his eloquence. He cocked his head sidelong, searching Caleb's face for some reaction. But Caleb only stared straight ahead, lost in a daydream. He imagined Sara running in the sun, bounding over obstacles while she chased deer and birds. Caleb almost drooled with the anticipation of disappearing into a place where he was the center of the world, free to howl at the moon.

"Well? C'mon, Cal. I have to get back soon."

Caleb squinted at Frazier, suddenly gripped by suspicion.

"If this place is so great, why not go yourself, why don't you want to stay there?"

"I don't like the boonies. I don't hike or bike or swim or tiptoe through the fucking tulips." He snickered. "Besides, there's no women. I like to be where the action is, you know what I mean?"

Caleb shrugged. Frazier's explanation was reasonable except for the fact that Caleb always suspected he was a closet homosexual. Still, it was a minor point. After all, Frazier would not be staying at the house with him.

A moment of silence passed while a wrinkled curtain of intense thought fell over Caleb's face.

"Sure, I'd love to go, Frazier," he announced with a broad smile.

Frazier patted him on the back and handed him a gold pen and a napkin. Caleb smiled while he scribbled down the directions, the thrill of an adventure long overdue pulsing through him like electricity, making his toes tingle.

"If you have any problems, Cal, call me on my cell phone, not at work. It's nobody else's business."

Moments later, Caleb shook Frazier's clammy hand once more and stumbled out into the night, intoxicated less with alcohol than with anticipation of a release from the shackles of the city and his half empty life.

Chapter 3

WHILE FRAZIER DROVE THROUGH the blackness, he wondered as he often did about the things his father spoke of over the phone in his office when he shut the soundproof door. Maybe he was connected to organized crime, or maybe he was a drug dealer planning a shipment from South America. In any event, Frazier was certain that the export business was only a façade used to disguise something far darker and infinitely more profitable.

Frazier wanted in on it for no other reason than he was outside of the loop.

Most of the time, Frazier sat at an empty desk and played solitaire on his computer. Occasionally, his father would drop a file on his desk and tell him to do something with it. Despite the fact that he was paid well for doing nothing, he had demanded to know what else went on when his father left the office for destinations unknown. His father only responded that one day, when Frazier had proven himself worthy, he would make him a part of the "dealings" that kept them so wealthy and comfortable.

But Frazier quickly grew tired of imagining a life that he was not absolutely sure he wanted to know anything about. He wanted to drink and fuck men and wear expensive clothes, nothing more. The only reason he ever confronted his father about it was because he resented the secrecy that made Frazier feel as if quarantined for having some contagious disease.

Frazier turned up the radio and lit a cigarette. He noticed that in the absence of any streetlights, the darkness was a vacuum, even snatching the glare from his headlights before it could reach the road ahead. But he was hardly concerned. As a teenager, Frazier had driven his father's car along these thin, winding roads so many times that he could anticipate the next sharp curve when he could not even distinguish the blacktop from the curtain of night. Each time the BMW settled down through a turn, Frazier guided it effortlessly through the familiar arc emerging without so much as even a chirp from the tires.

Frazier let the cigarette dangle from his mouth while he gripped the steering wheel with both hands. He imagined that he was thin, with a sculpted chin and piercing blue eyes that sucked people in to his witty dialogues. He imagined that he was nothing less than a movie star and that the mysterious tale of his life would be analyzed and recorded for posterity. He was a man on a secret mission. Everything had gone well so far, especially since Caleb Magellan was on board.

He patted his inside coat pocket to be sure the plane ticket was still there.

"Yes," Frazier whispered to himself.

This time he would follow his scowling father on his business for the sake of knowing. Maybe, he thought, he would confront him with what he learned about him just to piss him off, just to show his father that he had inherited some of his cleverness. Frazier smiled. The idea was brilliant. And Caleb Magellan unwittingly made it a reality. Frazier needed someone to stay in the New Jersey house while he was gone, if only to feed the horses and ward off the decay an empty house invites. Frazier had thought long and hard and decided that Caleb was the only person Frazier knew who did not despise him enough to steal anything or burn the house to the ground. Of course, it was no accident that Frazier had "bumped" into him in Philadelphia.

And hopefully, this was the last time he would have to make the two-hour drive to New Jersey for quite a long time.

On the next straightaway, while Frazier flicked his cigarette butt out the window, there was suddenly an explosion of light all around him, momentarily blinding him. He jammed on the brakes until his pupils adjusted to the brightness. A car was on his bumper behind him, flashing its high beams on and off in rapid succession. Then blue and red strobe lights pulsated, penetrating deeply into the bowels of the forest on either side of the road like laser beams. Frazier slowed to a stop and threw the shifter into park.

Before Frazier could even open his door, the police car smashed into him, pushing his car, its wheels whining in protest. He wanted to scream and curse, but he was frozen by the unprovoked violence of the attack. Each time a rational thought crept into his throbbing mind, another bone jarring jolt threw him against his seat then into the dashboard, turning his head into a boiling blob of panic. When Frazier finally managed to get the car into drive, it was already too late. He was delicately poised, balancing on an embankment that dropped away into a black hole where the slimy river waited for him.

Frazier thrust his head out of the window and looked back on his murderer. For some desperate reason, he decided that he had to see the face, if only to ask what he could have done to deserve a watery grave. Frazier craned his neck but he could only make out light and chrome and shadows. The last thing he saw as the car dove down, briefly suspended above the water, was the deep sky, indifferent to his struggle. The river welcomed him, its gritty ooze and mud spilling in, chasing out the air he reached and clawed for. Frazier's last thought was nothing more than a mental gasp, a rush of fear, despair and hatred because only then had he realized what a worthless man he had become.

Chapter 4

CALEB PACKED HIS THINGS in a large duffle bag while Sara watched him intently. Her head was tilted to one side and her long ears were pricked up and alert, giving her head a triangular shape that made it appear larger than it really was. She was aware that some event was about to take place that would interrupt her daily routine, and she was obviously concerned about whether or not she was included in the plans.

"Don't worry baby," he said reassuringly while he patted her head. "I won't leave you behind."

Caleb knew that she could not really understand what he said, but she obviously understood the meaning he conveyed through the tone of his voice because she wagged her tail and gently mouthed his hand, leaving it glistening with her saliva.

Caleb quickly tired in the heat and humidity that enveloped him like a damp blanket. He paused to wipe away some sweat that had started to drip from his forehead. Even his mind moved slowly, as if made rusty by the moisture. He examined the small piles of clothing on his bed to be sure he had not forgotten anything.

With the exception of one pair of jeans and a wool sweater, he decided he would take only summer clothing, shorts and T-shirts for the most part. Although it was only the first week in June, a heat wave bathed the region, drawing complaints from the same people who had only two months before been wishing for an early spring and warm weather.

When the bag was almost full, he packed it down to make room for his toiletries, which he had sealed in a plastic zip-loc bag. When he was finished, he set the duffle bag on the floor and studied it for a moment, appreciating its utility.

Caleb walked out into the living room and picked up the napkin on which he had scribbled the directions to Frazier's house the night before. He considered rewriting them more legibly on a blank piece of paper, but there was something romantic and intriguing about getting lost in the country. He secretly hoped the directions would blow away as he drove, forcing him to stop and ask for help from some colorful character at a greasy roadside diner.

As Caleb and Sara made their way the few blocks to the parking garage in the early light, Caleb watched people move about the streets on their way to jobs most of them probably hated. Their faces were devoid of any outward expression as they hurried. Perhaps, Caleb thought, they were tired of the mindless routine and wondered what their lives would be like if they stowed away on lumbering freight trains.

For the first time in recent memory, Caleb was not one of the masses. He shuddered to think of the precious time he wasted worrying about whether or not he was going to be late for things that hardly seemed important now.

They walked down the ramp into the garage. They moved past the daily spaces to the damp, dark bowels of the structure, where monthly customers were relegated. He had not driven his car in months, only raising the dust cover enough to allow him to get in and start it occasionally. He could hardly remember what the car looked like when completely exposed.

Caleb lifted the cover from the hood, then gently folded it back until the soft, sleek lines were revealed. The silver metallic finish sparkled even in the dim orange light, and he was once more reminded why he spent so much money over the years to have the powerful Stingray convertible restored to mint condition.

He ran his fingers along the lines of the fiberglass body and wondered how man could create anything so smooth and perfect before there were computers to perform the necessary calculations. He slowly walked around the car before opening the trunk, burning the image of its low-slung profile into his mind before he was actually behind the wheel where he could only imagine how the car looked as it weaved in and out of traffic.

He forced his duffle bag into the tiny trunk, put the top down and opened the passenger door so Sara could climb in. Although she had never ridden in the car before, she seemed to instantly understand her place as passenger. She sat quietly and stared ahead through the windshield, as if impatient to get under way.

Caleb slid in next her and shut the door. He turned the key and the beast roared to life. He gunned the engine several times. The sound of the tiny explosions that drove the pistons echoed throughout the garage, drowning out the engine noise of passing foreign cars whining in protest. Caleb took his foot off the gas pedal and the Stingray quieted, churning softly yet crisply, telling all that she was ready for a fight. He eased the car up the ramp and merged slowly with the morning commuter traffic.

For the better part of an hour, he was confined by the narrow city streets and rows of traffic lights that seemed to conspire against his freedom by glaring at him with their angry red eyes every time he approached.

Finally, they reached the open turnpike and Caleb pointed the car north. Caleb accelerated, synchronizing the clutch and gas pedal so the car shifted seamlessly through the gears. He passed by several cars that seemed to be standing still. The big V-8 snarled with impunity each time it consumed a victim, spitting out the carcass behind his car, where it disappeared along with the outline of the city in his rearview mirror.

He glanced over at Sara. Although she did not seem to notice, her pendulous ears caught the wind and flapped like wings with such intensity that he thought she might fly away. Caleb almost gave in to the impulse to smile and mockingly wave at the drivers headed into the city who were stopped in a perpetual traffic jam in the southbound lane.

When the ribbon of concrete was no longer bordered by an endless string of malls and countertop outlets, he slowed to a safe speed and some of his tension abated. Beyond the guardrail in the distance, opulent tract homes seemingly dropped from the sky were embedded in fields where farmers had once plowed and sweated. They were places where stifled people like himself woke up, sipped coffee, then drove almost an hour to get to the filthy city. It was hardly progress. The sight of the gaudy structures made him realize that there was really no happy medium between oppressive crowds and sweet country solitude.

For the next hour and a half, Caleb drove while the sun climbed high. He pretended his left hand was a wing that rose and fell in the rushing air outside the car. He was all but oblivious to the curious looks of the drivers he passed.

At least for the moment, he was as independent of his worries as the large birds he watched gliding in lazy circles near the horizon. It was as if the sun and wind and smooth hum of the engine worked together to hypnotize him, and lull him back to a time when he felt secure. For the first time in years, he was able to feel the joy and freedom of the light summer days of childhood, before his father injected poisonous fear and shame into his personality. But the softness in his chest was fleeting as the road ahead split and he was forced to concentrate on finding his way. He quickly pulled the directions from the glove box and deciphered them barely in time to make his exit.

Instantly, he was transported to a world that the twenty-first century somehow forgot. He found himself on a smooth, two-lane road barely wide enough to accommodate vehicles passing in opposite directions. As he rounded a gentle curve, he was welcomed to Sussex County,

New Jersey, by a shiny brass placard with raised lettering adorning a wooden fence post with understated elegance.

The smell of fresh cow manure and heat filled his nostrils, reminding him that the patchwork quilt of green fields in the distance was actually farmed. Unlike the dead brown land he had passed through, this soil was writhing with carefully nurtured life. Sara too had awakened, confronted with a smorgasbord of stimuli. She raised her nose in the air and snorted, trying to understand and evaluate the microscopic particles that tickled her sensitive palate like a fine perfume.

Caleb was familiar with the less-than-kind references to New Jersey. He had heard it called the "armpit of the nation" and the "the country's largest landfill." But the serenity he found here was a world, no, a universe, apart from crowded cities like Newark, Elizabeth or Jersey City. In fact, he could never have before imagined the charming softness of the vast countryside hidden away in the most densely populated state in the country.

They passed a dirt road leading to a stone farmhouse with a slate roof. The dark gray and brown stone highlighted the few pieces of white trim around the windows and doorways that shone brightly in the sun. A well-manicured lawn stretched to the road before it like a lush green carpet. Just beyond the house was a large barn painted the traditional crimson that could be seen for several miles on a cloudy day. Some cows lingered in a nearby field, their heads lowered while they fed on grass in the shade of a copse of trees. With the exception of a rusting tractor parked next to the barn, the portrait of this land had probably changed little over the past two hundred years.

The green openness disappeared as the road suddenly wound sharply through thick forest along the contours of the Delaware River. On either side of the road, sturdy oaks and maples mingled with fragrant pine and spruce to cast a perpetual shadow across the macadam where the air was cool and still. Occasionally, Caleb caught glimpses of the sparkling river reflecting the sun through narrow gaps between the trees.

As he rounded a particularly sharp curve, he came to an intersection where a rusting steel bridge spanned the river into the forest on the other side, and provided a majestic view of the waterway as it subtly cut through the thickly wooded terrain. Just before the bridge sat a small log cabin. Its roof extended out past the entrance to form a covered porch. A carved wooden sign hung down from the side of the building and read simply "General Store."

Caleb downshifted and pulled the Stingray into the dirt parking lot so he could study the directions. Frazier's words were clear: turn left on Jenny Gap Road, at the old Riverton Bridge. Although the road ahead was not marked, this was most likely the intersection Frazier spoke of. But the lack of a road sign gave Caleb an excuse to inquire in the store for directions and sample the local culture.

Caleb climbed out of the car and stretched his legs, then let Sara out on the leash. Although she was usually obedient, Caleb was not sure how she would react to the wilderness. He closed the convertible top before putting her back into the car for fear that she might disappear into the forest in response to instincts awakened by the strange environment.

On the porch of the tiny store, Caleb found Mason jars filled with preserves and vegetables arranged neatly in rows on wooden crates. There were also buckets of fresh apples, grapes and ears of corn for sale. He opened the screen door and stepped into the dark cabin that smelled of dust and wood smoke. When his eyes adjusted to the low light, he could see jars of peppermint sticks, honey and beef jerky arranged on shelves along the bare walls. In the center of the room was a display of wine apparently produced locally. It was an odd mixture of fresh produce and imported tourist fancies packaged in such a way as to suggest local origin. Nevertheless, it reminded him of old black and white photographs, and he felt instantly at ease.

"That's a beautiful car you have out there."

Caleb turned. A short, elderly man with wisps of gray corn silk for hair seemed to have appeared out of thin air behind him. He was wearing a dirty pair of denim overalls with a white button-down shirt underneath. His ensemble was topped off with a crooked red bow tie. He looked as though he were undecided as to whether he should go to work or go to church.

The old man squinted behind round, wire-rimmed glasses, indicating that the prescription was no longer strong enough to compensate for his degenerating vision.

"It's a '67, right?" he asked while he pulled a rag from his back pocket and lightly dabbed his forehead.

"That's right."

"I knew it," he said excitedly, as if to congratulate himself that his mind had not completely failed him. "I used to have one just like it."

Caleb imagined the old man behind the wheel, barely able to see the road over his huge bowtie. He had to use all of his will to hold back a chuckle.

"Don't you laugh," the old man warned while waving a crooked finger, "that was before I got old." Then he smiled. For a moment, the wrinkles disappeared and Caleb could picture in his mind the chiseled face of the strong young man he used to be. "Now, sir," he asked while he stuffed the rag back into his pocket, "what can I do for you?"

"I'm looking for Jenny Gap Road, have you heard of it?"

"Sure," he said while he motioned back toward the door. "Just go to the intersection out here, then make a left, that's Jenny Gap."

"I appreciate it."

The old man folded his arms and waited. It was clear that his assistance was not free.

"I guess…I mean I want to buy something from you too. I haven't eaten all day."

"It's all good," he muttered while surveying the contents of room, "but it's not right for a meal, only snacking, that sort of thing." He turned back to Caleb and gently took him by the elbow and began to lead him to the back of the store. "I'll tell you what, I'll share my lunch with you, and you'll buy some fruit and a bottle of wine before you leave."

Caleb wanted to resist, he wanted to walk out of the store and get back in his car. He was conditioned by television and newspapers to be wary of the kindness of others for fear they harbored some darker motive. Sensing his reluctance, the old man stopped and examined Caleb over the top of his glasses.

"You haven't been out past the smog and horns for a while," he said as if he understood that when people lived together like sardines they developed an unconscious contempt for each other. "Out here, most people don't even lock their doors, even when they're not home."

Caleb was suddenly embarrassed. He cursed himself for being so pessimistic that he could not even look the old man in the eye.

"I'm sorry...you know, the fresh air takes some getting used to."

"Hello, Sorry." The old man laughed and extended a trembling hand. "I'm Pete, Pete Barry."

Caleb took his hand firmly and felt taught, callous patches of skin he imagined had probably been toughened by swinging an ax or carrying heavy objects around the store. Caleb smiled. He understood that this simple, trusting man probably had much more to fear from an outsider than anyone passing through had to fear from him. He was the kind of man Caleb wished would die rather than understand how cruel the society was that threatened his peace.

"I'm Caleb Magellan, and I'm more or less just passing through."

"C'mon Caleb," he said, once more leading him by the arm, "we'll go sit down by the river."

On their way out the back of the store, Pete picked up a small plastic cooler sitting on the floor near the door. Outside, he led Caleb down a flight of rickety wooden steps all but overgrown with a thick cover of green vegetation that somehow took root on the steep, sandy bank. Pete whistled the theme song from Oklahoma as he slowly dropped down, careful to avoid getting ensnared by long, prickly weeds sprouting through gaps in the steps like the tentacles of an octopus.

They reached the bottom and stood on a large flat rock extending a few feet into the river, forming a natural dock. Pete opened the cooler and removed a plain brown paper bag. He closed the lid and sat down on it, using it as a makeshift stool. Caleb followed his lead and sat down on the sun-baked stone next to him.

"I hope you like peanut butter and jelly," Pete said while he pulled a sandwich wrapped in plastic from the paper bag.

Caleb nodded, and Pete handed him half of the sandwich that had been neatly cut diagonally. It had been a long time since Caleb experienced the sweet yet salty flavor of peanut butter and jelly together. He wondered how two foods, neither of which by itself was particularly interesting, could combine to form such a tasty meal. Maybe it was simply because he was hungry, or maybe it was that when he closed his eyes, the sticky consistency of the stuff clinging to the roof of his mouth reminded him of a time when he traded the contents of his Starsky and Hutch lunch box with his friends and thought that babies were made when a man and a woman kissed too long. When the sandwich was gone, he licked his fingers and wished he had more.

"My wife and I bought this place after I retired ten years ago," Pete began while he handed Caleb some saltines from a small plastic bag. "We used to live in Hoboken. I worked in New York City, in a factory. We always dreamed about getting out and living in the country. So, when we saw the ad in the newspaper that this place was for sale, we packed our bags and never worried whether or not we could make it work. As it turned out we did alright, on account of there's some family YMCA camps up the road here, and the campers stop by here all through the summer."

"What about the winter?" Caleb asked between mouthfuls.

"Well, we bought a cottage real cheap just on the other side of the bridge there in Pennsylvania, and the money we made during the camp season was just enough to get us through."

Pete stopped eating and let his hands rest on his knees, still clutching part of his sandwich. He gazed longingly out across the water.

"My wife died, it's been almost a year now," he sighed, obviously still trying to convince himself of her passing.

Caleb could not think of anything to say that would not seem to trivialize the old man's turmoil, so he looked out across the river too, and tried to imagine what made Pete recall the death of his partner. Maybe it was the sound of the current whispering along the smooth rocks lining the shore, or the hot wind blowing through the trees, making their leaves flutter like millions of butterflies. Perhaps, he thought, it was the smell of rotting mud and new flowers that made Pete wonder about the contradiction of life, that she was gone, and he, like the spring growth, had been reborn to a different world.

"So," Pete inquired cheerfully while he finished his lunch, never hinting that he had slipped back in time for those few quiet minutes, "what brings you up here?"

Caleb recounted the entire tale excitedly, even to the point of describing the eccentric egomaniac, Frazier McCoy. But when he was finished, Pete did not laugh at Caleb's enthusiasm or remark that Promise was a beautiful place filled with friendly people who would try to convince him to stay there. Strangely, Pete said nothing at all, and Caleb thought that he offended him somehow during the story.

"I should tell you," he spoke finally, sounding distant and afraid, "they don't like strangers up there."

Caleb cocked his head, confused by the vague warning.

"What do you mean?"

"It's a little town filled with rich people who drive by here sometimes in their expensive cars and look at me and my customers like we're dog shit."

Caleb chimed in. "Well, locals never like the tourists, right?"

"It's more than that. They don't even slow down when there's people around the store. You gotta get out of their way or be run down." Pete paused and took a deep breath. "I called the county Sheriff, Millstone is his name, to complain. He came down here and told me to keep my mind on my business, that they can do what they want, and so can he. Then the bastard said to me if I keep bugging him, I could have an accident. I was so scared, I didn't say nothing back. I just stood there and nodded. Then he left, but not before that bastard snatched one of my apples."

Caleb raised his eyebrows briefly in response. He thought perhaps the old man was exaggerating, or that a contempt for the well-to-do, a fading memory and a breakdown in communication had combined to create his perception that he was being threatened. Caleb found it hard to believe that anyone in this lazy countryside could be so vicious, or that there was anything out in the woods or hills that was worth killing someone over.

"Pete, are you sure you didn't just misunderstand him?"

"No, godammit," he snapped while he abruptly stood up and picked up the cooler. "I know what I heard and what I seen. And I'll tell you, he meant it."

"Look Pete, I'm not trying to upset you, I'm just saying it's hard for me to believe, that's all."

"Well, believe it."

Caleb trailed behind him silently back up the stairs and into the cabin. He watched while Pete returned the cooler to its place on the floor, then pulled the rag from his back pocket and tried to wipe his stiff hands clean.

"I'm sorry," he whispered without turning to face Caleb, who still remained in the doorway, unsure whether he was still welcome. "I shouldn't have got pissed at you, it would be hard for anyone to understand."

"This sheriff, what was his name again?" Caleb asked.

"Millstone, I don't know his first name. It doesn't much matter anyway, I guess. Why don't you come in here and pick out some stuff, help keep an old man in business."

Pete turned around and squinted, managing to smile once more. Caleb walked in and gave him a pat on his back as he passed. He picked up a bottle of wine and put some apples in a brown paper bag Pete handed to him from behind the counter. He put the goods down next to the old manual cash register. "Just like you said Pete, some fruit and a bottle of wine."

"That's good stuff," Pete remarked, gesturing toward the dark bottle with his head while he pushed tabs on the register that clicked and chattered in response. Pete handed Caleb a part of a matchbook with a phone number scribbled on it. "That's just in case you have need of a friendly face while you're up there in Promise. God knows you'll be plenty bored if you have to rely on any of those snobs for conversation."

Just then, the door to the store slowly opened. A man, obviously of Asian decent, quickly stepped inside. Caleb's eyes widened. The man was wearing a flowing orange robe that extended down to the tops of his shoes, which Caleb could not otherwise make out. This gave one the impression that he was gliding along on a cushion of air. His hair was cut closely to the skin, leaving only a dark stubble as long as the two days of growth on Caleb's face. His eyes were large, round and deep, like an old well. Caleb glanced over at Pete, who smiled warmly. He bowed slightly. "Master Kim, it is always a pleasure."

The man bowed slowly in return, his palms pressed together in front of him as if praying.

"Mr. Barry," the man spoke gently, "we hope all is well with you."

The man turned to Caleb and repeated the motion. Caleb nodded.

"Mr. Kim, this is my new friend Caleb. Caleb, this is Mr. Kim, he's one of the Buddhist monks at Hilldale Retreat. You probably passed the driveway a mile or so back, but you wouldn't know it, it's not very well marked. They don't want any tourists."

Mr. Kim turned to Caleb and explained. "I don't wish for you to misunderstand. We do not hide ourselves away, but we simply do not advertise our presence either. We attempt to eliminate as much distraction as possible so we might better concentrate on our studies. However, sir, if ever you desire to visit us, you are always welcome. That is our way."

Mr. Kim did not wait for a response, but turned back to Pete.

"I'm afraid we need some things. Do you have any rice left since the last time I was here?"

"Of course, I have a bunch of it behind the counter. I keep it just for you."

Pete bent down, and began to pile small paper sacks on the counter. "Just give me a minute, I'll get the rest of it from out back."

When Pete disappeared, Mr. Kim turned once more to Caleb.

"I sense that you are curious about me, what I and my brothers do."

In fact, Caleb was intensely curious. He had studied religion in college, as everyone was required to do, but remembered little about Buddhism. He recalled Karma and reincarnation and the statues of the pudgy, contemplative Buddha. But Caleb sensed in this man a deep peace and contentment, a quality he never gleaned from his studies.

"Well...a bit, yes," he admitted.

The slightly built man smiled broadly, then softly applauded, clapping his hands together quickly several times.

"Good, good. You are courageous to admit your interest despite knowing little of our quest. That is a very good sign. It warms my heart to know that others are still open to a different way of living. You see, curiosity leads to tolerance, then acceptance, then peace and freedom from suffering.

"To one such as you, the core belief of Buddhism is best stated as the search to free ourselves from the cycle of human suffering by enlightenment. To be enlightened, explained plainly, is to see and understand the one thing that does not change, awareness. To be so aware, one's mind must be free of all distraction, free of all wants, needs and material pursuits."

Caleb's boggled mind felt like it was bouncing around the inside of his skull. His rational logical side sought to fit together words like a puzzle, to add it all up and come out with the right number, but he knew somewhere deep inside that it had nothing to do with logic at all. It had to do with understanding who he really was, and that he was nothing at all. And he had to admit to himself that the idea of letting everything go was one he had always contemplated, but he had never realized there was a discipline of the mind devoted to just such an endeavor. It was actually frightening.

"I see," whispered Mr. Kim. "I see it in your bright eyes, the seed has been planted in just these few moments. Let this seed grow and you will begin to ask many questions. And when you seek answers, if you do, I will make myself available to you."

Out of sheer respect for such a thoughtful man, Caleb bowed. He was truly humbled by his profound words.

"I appreciate your time," he whispered. "I'm staying up the road in Promise for a while. I'll think about the things you said."

"Promise?" said Mr. Kim. "How ironic." His eyes narrowed. He drew a step closer to Caleb while he spoke. "Did you ever hear the word 'Samsara'?"

Caleb shook his head. "No."

"It refers to what we perceive as our reality. It refers to all your yearning for material things. It also refers to emotion, ambition, drive for success. It refers to all those things that are really nothing at all. These wants and needs are things we create which only distract us from realizing our true, peaceful nature. These wants and needs are things that make you judge others to hide your own failings. These things make you hate others."

"I got it all now," Pete bellowed cheerfully as he returned. "Can you handle these bags, Mr. Kim?"

"I can."

Mr. Kim handed Pete some money.

"I'll have some more in for you next week if you want it, Mr. Kim."

"And I will return if we are in need, Mr. Barry."

Mr. Kim smiled at Pete, then turned and curtly bowed to both Pete and Caleb. Caleb nodded once more as Mr. Kim passed on his way out of the store. He watched as Mr. Kim loaded his groceries into the back of a plain white minivan, then drove away.

Caleb noticed that Pete was standing next to him.

"Mr. Kim is a gentleman," he remarked, "a true gentleman."

"What have I stumbled into here, Pete?" Caleb asked rhetorically. "Strange towns, the super rich and Buddhist monks?"

Pete laughed heartily. "Welcome to New Jersey."

Caleb gathered his things and prepared to leave. Just as he got to the door, he turned back.

"Hey Pete, maybe you can show me how to fish while I'm here, I mean if you have some time."

"Just swing by the store," Pete offered as he held the door, "or give me a call, I'll have plenty of free time until the camps open up again in about a month."

Caleb shook his hand firmly and turned to leave.

"Watch out for yourself," Pete added as Caleb was halfway out the door. "It never hurts to keep your eyes open."

"Okay Pete."

Caleb pulled the Stingray through the dirt lot. In his rear view mirror he could see a trail of dust billow out from behind the car until his wheels gripped the black road. He accelerated through the intersection, turning left on Jenny Gap Road, yet another macadam path that randomly twisted and turned like an ancient vine.

As he passed down the highway in the cool shade of the forest, he thought about Pete and about growing old and ornery. Certainly the sheriff had said something that Pete thought was disrespectful, but he knew that older people had a tendency to mull trivial things over in their minds until the matters became all-consuming. Caleb could hardly believe that anyone could threaten the life of old Pete, especially because he only complained about some reckless drivers. Caleb told himself that none of it really mattered anyway, because he was actually invited into this town by one of its residents, and he was sure to receive little resistance. But as Caleb bit into one of the sweet fresh apples, part of which he fed to Sara, who had been staring at him anxiously until she received her share, he knew that he would keep his eyes open. After all, as the saying goes, forewarned is forearmed. Besides, any man who sold such perfect fruit was someone who knew his business and had to be taken at his word.

Ahead, through the next curve, the road cut straight through a clearing where the ground and humid air reflected a hazy, yellow glow. He pulled his sunglasses down off his forehead as he glided out from beneath the trees. He welcomed the warmth on his face. On either side were the remnants of an old cemetery, which explained the absence of trees in the otherwise dense forest.

The thin gray stones leaned to and fro, some at such extreme angles that Caleb wondered what anchored them against gravity. Others were broken, but the wind and rain had smoothed the fractures.

Strangely, a black, wrought-iron fence with almost no rusty decay enclosed the cemetery. The lawn too was well manicured, soft and green, the very living antithesis of the dead, blemished stones. The place seemed to whisper to Caleb, to suggest that he should understand that death was as old as life, and that he might be interested in the tidbits of history the granite would reveal.

Caleb downshifted and pulled the car onto the narrow shoulder. After he had put Sara on a leash, they stood in the middle of the road while Caleb decided which portion of the cemetery to visit.

They strolled across the highway and Caleb lifted the latch on the gate. It was well oiled, and swung open silently. With Sara leading the way, he waded among the knee-high stones.

The first monument with a legible inscription revealed that a man named Thomas Smithy was lying underneath. He was born in 1804 and died in 1868. Another stone farther down the row recorded the death of Ann Zeiger, who died in 1865 at the age of forty-two. Her husband was buried next to her, and was only fifty years old when he breathed his last. Considering the dates and names that he could read with the naked eye, he could only guess at the age of the stones whose inscriptions had long been washed away by time.

In the last row of graves, protected by the branches of a massive oak that was no doubt only a sapling when the cemetery saw its first inhabitants, Caleb found some tombstones in far better condition. He was drawn to one in particular. It contained what appeared to be a lengthy epitaph to the individual, and he dropped down on one knee in order to read it.

> Here lies Christiana Morgan,
> aged 13 years and 3 months
> upon her death in this year,
> Eighteen Hundred and Seventy Two.
> Gone is the voice that once filled our house with
> laughter. Gone too is the smile of the girl who for us was
> the incarnation of the joy and innocence of our youth.
> Empty is her chair and the place we set at the table.
> Empty too is the now stale air that once was thick with
> her contagious, boundless exuberance.
> Dark now is her room and those hidden corners in the
> garden where she played. Dark too are our hearts, now
> that she has been so suddenly whisked away and walks
> in the night sky without us.

Caleb immediately sensed the grief of the family who knew the girl and nurtured her, only to see her life abruptly snuffed out. More profoundly, the simple words provided a glimpse into the lives of people who struggled and were all but forgotten these many years later.

While he pondered his own brief existence in these terms, he sat down on the grass and closed his eyes. He pretended that he was a living tombstone, a breathing memorial to his own life who stood on busy street corners and bellowed the details of the things he had accomplished, or failed to realize, to anyone who was interested. In this way, he could assure that at least some people might understand him before he was gone, before the task of expressing himself was left to strangers.

Caleb shaded his eyes. In the distance, on the far, opposite side of the cemetery, a miniature obelisk pierced the shadow of a tall, gangly tulip tree. It was by far the largest monument, perhaps twenty-five feet high. A marble fence about a foot high surrounded it. Naturally, he moved toward it to discover what person or family deserved such reverence. He noted that the faces of all the other headstones looked upon the obelisk like orderly, obedient soldiers, forever prostrate before their general.

Caleb only got close enough to make out the name before the phallic monster called on its dead troops.

The faint whisper he thought he only imagined when he first looked on the cemetery began to well up around him. It started softly, like the wind blowing through the trees in the forest beyond, or a light rain falling and spotting the ground. Soon, the hiss became almost deafening, and he whirled around wildly, convinced that some poisonous snake was poised to strike at his flesh. He glanced at Sara, and she too stood tensely, scanning the terrain for the source of the terrible noise. Suddenly the static faded and was replaced by what seemed to be human sounds and words uttered by a thousand invisible people at the same time, all competing for his attention. He thought he could make out sad wails, promises of love, nervous laughter and desperate gasps. He covered his ears and heard himself scream at the voices to be quiet, to dissipate back into the air. Once more, the sound faded, and was replaced by sweet silence.

Caleb stumbled to the gate and raised his face to the sun, shading his eyes with a trembling hand. He asked the sky if he were going insane. But Caleb remembered Sara's reaction to the strange noise. Even now, she circled him slowly, warning off the unseen intruder with a low throaty growl, and he knew that it was not simply a product of his own imagination. Still, Caleb could not allow himself to believe anything more than some form of the heat and wind and moisture had combined to create a strange, yet fully explainable phenomenon. He convinced himself that somewhere a scientist with thick glasses and pronounced teeth could diagram the whole thing for him. Caleb was sure the phenomenon even had a name. He decided that nature had belched and he chanced to be in the right place at the right time to experience the strange atmospheric anomaly.

Even as they were driving away, and the small clearing disappeared behind him when he rounded the next curve, Caleb did not wonder about the voices, which were best forgotten in any event, but was dreaming again about solitude.

Chapter 5

A T FIRST GLANCE, THE town of Promise seemed perfect and pure, the very stuff of a Norman Rockwell painting. Caleb found himself on a two-lane street that lazily circled a grassy island. In the center of the island the bronze statue of man pointed north with a strong outstretched arm and extended finger. His head was turned away, as if looking back upon a large crowd of people gathered behind him. His lips were parted as if to command them to follow him whatever may happen. An elderly couple was seated at one of the ornate cast iron benches surrounding the figure along a brick walkway. They watched and laughed as a young boy, perhaps their grandson, ran back and forth in the grass, trying to drag a blue and yellow box kite into the breeze.

Across the street, various shops were arranged around the circle. Each one was painted the same stark, sanitary white and glowed brightly in the afternoon sun. Most had striped black and white awnings that cast shadows over the display windows underneath. Caleb could see some cars moving around him, BMWs and Mercedes mostly, parking in front of the stores in spaces neatly designated with fresh lines of yellow paint.

Figures moved slowly along the sidewalk and in and out of the stores. They greeted each other and nodded or sometimes stopped to shake hands. A mail carrier leaned against one of the iron street lamps that resembled old gaslights while he sorted some envelopes. Caleb noticed a woman wearing a tailored linen suit herding several giggling children with ice cream cones out of a building with the words "Pharmacy and Fountain" embroidered in gold lettering on the front of the awning. Caleb slowed the car to a crawl while she held open the door to a Range Rover and the children climbed in.

Caleb pulled the Stingray into the spot next to her. The woman noticed him just as she was about to pull her car door shut. He could tell she was examining him from behind her sunglasses. She was blonde, slender and tan. Judging by the fit and style of her clothes, Caleb guessed that she probably had never even been in the parking lot of a K-Mart. He turned the car off, and inhaled deeply, taking in the scent of hot pavement and fresh grass clippings.

For no other reason than to enjoy the light and wind and sheer quiet beauty of the town, Caleb strolled past the shops, sometimes leaning close to the glass to block the glare from the windows so he could see what was offered for sale. He passed a gourmet food shop, then a dry cleaner. He stopped to examine a gray three-button suit in the window of a men's clothing store. *It was on sale for $1700.00.* He pressed his face against the glass. A thin middle-aged man was on the phone behind the counter with his back to the door. He was twirling the end of a measuring tape while he spoke.

Caleb stepped back and examined the storefront, then glanced over his shoulder at the rest of the buildings. With the exception of a church steeple piercing the sky in the distance, they were all the same. Each was a perfectly maintained two-story, clapboard building with flower boxes under each of the second floor windows, from which sprouted colorful annuals. Even the narrow dark alleys in between seemed to be swept clean of cigarette butts and other loose garbage.

Caleb followed the scent of boiling grease and barbeque to the

building next door. The awning read, "Stonewall's Diner." He pushed
open the door. A bell jingled somewhere. The chatter from the counter
and the tables trailed off as he made his way to an open booth against
the wall. He nodded politely at the faces that turned to study him as
he passed. After he sat down, the conversations resumed, but only in
hushed tones.

A scowling waitress in a white uniform and white shoes waited on
the people in the booth next to his. A man dressed casually in khakis
and a white button-down shirt was on a cell phone. He cupped his hand
over the receiver while he explained to the waitress that he wanted an
open face turkey sandwich, no mashed potatoes. Caleb noticed a gold
Rolex watch on his wrist very similar to the one Frazier was wearing.
The waitress nodded, then disappeared behind a swinging door into the
kitchen.

Three women seated at the counter sipped coffee and laughed. Bags
filled with purchases sat on the floor at their feet. At one of the tables,
a younger man in a black turtleneck read a newspaper with his legs
crossed while a girl, perhaps six or seven years old, nibbled on a grilled
cheese sandwich, drawing on the paper placemat with a crayon between bites. At another table, two gray haired men in wool suits argued
over something. One of them kept throwing up his hands to express his
frustration. Some other people came and left, each waving to those who
were seated, or patting them on the backs or telling them they would
see them on the golf course.

Maybe it was the way the looks exchanged between these people
lingered just a bit too long. Or maybe it was the fact that a simple pat
on the shoulder led to an almost imperceptible squeeze or affection-
ate rub. Caleb could not put his finger on what bothered him about the
people or this town except that it struck him as incestuous, as if there
was a bond far darker and deeper between them than mere neighborly
affection. He also felt their eyes on his back. Although no person had
openly stared at him since he sat down, he had the distinct feeling they

were watching him, averting their eyes when he happened to glance at any one of them.

After ten minutes, with no waitress in sight, Caleb grew impatient. He craned his neck to see over the top of the booth. He could make out several people scurrying about with pots and steaming food in the kitchen through a sliding wooden panel in the wall behind the counter.

A streak of light and flowing color moved in the kitchen. Caleb half stood up for a better view. He saw it again. A girl, maybe a young woman, wearing a sundress with a flower pattern twirled in a strange dance. Her raven black hair billowed out behind her like the sail on a graceful ship. She came back into view, spun once more and stopped, facing Caleb. Initially, she blushed, but slowly she smiled innocently and winked one of her brown eyes at Caleb, teasing him. He smiled. Now he was the one who blushed. A moment later, she was standing at his table.

"I'm sorry, I didn't mean to stare...I was just looking for the waitress."

She smiled with pouty lips and sat down on the other side of the table. She leaned her elbows on the table, then cradled her face with her hands. Caleb smelled sweat and lavender in her wake.

"I think that you were the one out of sorts," she teased in a thick southern accent that reminded him of swamps and alligators. "I guess I caught you."

Caleb laughed aloud.

"Maybe you did."

The girl leaned back and examined him with her dark eyes. She smiled once more then squinted and cocked her head quizzically.

"By the looks of you, I'd say you're visitin', or maybe you're just lost. Either way, you should get on outta' here, outta' this place."

Caleb was silent for a moment while he stared into her eyes, like pools of black rainwater that gave no hint of their depth. She was beautiful in a young, natural and unrefined way, but he could tell she was filled with a curiosity of adult pursuits. He noticed that her breasts pulled the thin dress taut across her chest when she breathed. He felt ashamed of himself for looking.

"How old are you?" he asked, then reconsidered the question. "I mean…do you work here?"

"I'm eighteen yesterday. I don't work here though, in this place, I work cleaning houses and such. But I have today off. My mama, she's the waitress here, but she's out smoking a cigarette right now."

"What's your name?"

"Trinity."

"I'm Caleb. Do you live here, in Promise?"

She shook her head back and forth in an exaggerated way, like a little girl.

"I can't tell you where I live."

Once more, Caleb was embarrassed.

"I'm sorry, I'm a stranger, you don't have to tell me anything."

Trinity grasped his right hand between both of her own. He could feel rough, parched skin, far older than her years.

"Oh no, it's not that I don't want to tell ya', its just that I can't tell, I'm not allowed." Trinity released him then motioned for him to lean closer. He turned his head and she whispered in his ear. "I'm here every Saturday, with my mom. You can come visit here if you like."

Suddenly, Trinity whimpered. Caleb looked up at the scowling waitress who had her by the arm.

"Is she botherin' you?" She's not supposed to be out here with the customers," she grunted in the same smoky, southern drawl as Trinity.

"No, not at all, she was just keeping me company until you got back."

"Well then, what can I get for you?"

"Just some coffee, to go, please. Here's five dollars, keep the change."

Trinity looked back over her shoulder and smiled once more while her mother dragged her off to the kitchen. It was then that Caleb noticed that she limped, that one of her legs was stiff and shiny, a prosthetic limb.

Caleb walked across the street toward the monument while he thought about Trinity. He felt sorry for her, but he felt more sorry for himself. She was confident and amiable despite the fact that she was poor, uneducated and missing a limb. He had almost every advantage, yet he whined to himself about what he had become and what he should have been. He cursed himself for being so selfish and oblivious. He thought about what Mr. Kim said. There had to be a better way, a way to let go of it all.

Caleb sat on one of the benches and sipped coffee in the shadow of the pointing statue. He leaned forward to read a brass plaque bolted to the concrete base. It stated that the image depicted Marcus McCoy. In 1863, he uprooted an entire town in Virginia and founded it here away from the Civil War, hence the name "Promise." He built an agricultural empire in the North that he shared with all the town's residents who followed him. The plaque also stated that he denounced slavery and the Confederate cause.

Caleb found the history fascinating. He was certain that Frazier was a direct descendent of Marcus McCoy, which would explain his family's wealth. It might also explain the wealth that saturated this all too perfect place. Still, he did not think that a common history alone was sufficient to explain the strange closeness he sensed between the people here. In any event, he decided to research the subject in more detail during his visit.

When Caleb finished the coffee, he walked back across the street to his car. He started the engine, studied the directions for a moment, then threw the car into reverse. He looked over his shoulder but his path was blocked and he had to jam on the brakes. It was a sheriff's car. A man wearing a cowboy style hat and sunglasses was looking directly at him. He was talking into his two-way radio. Caleb could read his lips enough to know that he was calling in his license plate number. *He was running*

his plate for no reason! Caleb wondered if this was Millstone, the man
Pete had mentioned.

The man stared unflinchingly at Caleb until the radio crackled again.
He dipped his head in response to what he heard, as if disappointed that
he would have no reason to roust an otherwise peaceful stranger. Caleb
shook his head in disgust. When he glanced behind him once more, the
car was gone, so quickly that he wondered if he had not imagined the
entire thing.

Intrigued, Caleb cruised along some of the residential blocks outside
the town proper. As he expected, he found quiet streets lined with blos-
soming trees shading thick green lawns. Mansions of widely differing
styles were restored meticulously to their looming glory.

He passed a white, two-story palace. Four massive Doric columns
supported its porch and veranda. Next door, separated by a row of massive oaks, stood a Victorian home with stained glass windows and twin
parapets capped with gleaming bronze. A half-circle driveway allowed
vehicles to approach and depart the property without being forced to back
up or turn around. Still another house was constructed of large square
stones arched in places to form windows and doorways. It reminded him
of no particular style, but of a medieval castle.

Even more astounding than the pristine condition of the dwellings was
the particular attention paid to their landscapes. Gardens of flowers surrounded each goliath with a ring of exploding color, like a sort of moat.
But the flowers were not randomly placed; rather each plant seemed to
be intentionally juxtaposed against the other to produce the most awe-in-
spiring affect. This no doubt required constant physical effort on a grand
scale.

When he turned a corner, Caleb witnessed a small army at work. At
least eight dirty, sweating men were busy either weeding, dumping mulch
or gathering debris. They were white, black and Hispanic, unshaven and
sinewy, dressed in dirty jeans or torn coveralls. Two of the men had paused
to share a cigarette. But when they saw Caleb's car, their eyes widened
and they quickly snatched the nearest tool, pretending to have been at

work all the while. *Why were they so frightened?* Caleb could not understand. Where he came from, laborers were defiantly lazy on the job, as if it was their right to linger and bitch about the heat and their hangovers.

No, Caleb decided, this was not like any other town he had ever seen. It was so ordered and ideal that even the light seemed to cooperate, filtering through to the ground in a soft, angelic glow.

Uneasy, he made his way back to the road that wound along the river, back to the natural world.

Chapter 6

HE DROVE THROUGH THE forest once again for several miles, thankful for the solitude and the wind that seemed to clear his mind. He drove past elaborate wrought iron gates and stone pillars that marked entrances to private estates artfully hidden deep in the trees. Caleb imagined that if he could fly over the land in a helicopter, he would see the rolling hills pock-marked with square lawns and sprawling stone mansions.

He rounded a sharp curve that demanded his full attention to avoid skidding off the road, and began to climb a long, gradual incline. He noticed two cast iron lanterns, replicas of old street lamps, off to the side of the road, marking his destination just as Frazier had promised. Caleb slowed the car, threading it through the narrow gap between the lamps and onto the driveway covered with loose, white stone.

Instantly, he was stricken with the vague feeling that he had passed down this road many, many times. Because the driveway sloped downward slightly, Caleb put the Stingray in neutral and let it coast quietly while he took in the mysterious beauty of the terrain.

On both sides of the approach, enormous oak and tulip trees stood two stories tall, towering over the driveway as if guarding against some enemy's approach. They appeared as if they might awaken from their ages old slumber at any moment to smother him with their long, heavy branches. Their tops formed a green canopy over him that seemed impervious to the elements. Between the trees, Caleb could see a green lawn that stretched about a quarter of a mile to the dark forest in the distance.

Ahead, a strange mist lingered across his path where the driveway leveled off around a bend. It obscured the rays of the sun until they reached the ground as only a dull gray light. For a moment, Caleb was blinded as he passed through the veil of moisture gathered on his windshield. The dampness wicked up the sweet smell of fresh cut grass and moist earth, punctuated by the spicy scents of other plants and flowers he could not identify, but which seemed as familiar as the smell of his own bed.

Caleb leaned his head out the window to get a better view of the road and to be sure he had not drifted off the driveway toward some hazard. A mountain of a house materialized in front of him, encompassing his entire field of vision. He stopped the car where the road ended in a cul-de-sac the size of the circle in town.

The white antebellum mansion glistened in the light, shining like a legendary castle of silver. It was as if an historical, gracious southern home that once dominated the steamy plantations of the South before the Civil War had been transplanted, brick by brick, in this unlikely location.

A series of wide, marble steps, flanked on either side by gnarled rose bushes, led visitors up to a cavernous porch running the length of the house. Four massive Doric columns supported the roof and an identical porch on the second floor. Perhaps twice the size and twice as sensual as any home in town, it was on the order of Tara. Caleb half expected to see women on the porches in lacy gowns with curly locks, trailed by eager young men dressed in Confederate uniforms, each waiting for the opportunity to impress the women with stories of bravery in battle.

On either side of the house was a neat row of weeping willow trees as tall as the house itself, strategically placed it seemed, to cloak the house with their long tendrils from any angle except the intended approach. Beyond them, the lawn separated the grounds from the wilderness.

To the right of the cul-de-sac where Caleb stood, a narrow gravel path led to a gray painted barn about a hundred yards away. Several horses were grazing lazily in a fenced pasture adjacent to their dwelling, refusing to acknowledge his presence.

Behind him, he could see a small lake in the distance beyond the driveway, down a grassy slope. Past that, more black forest stretched to the horizon, reminding him of the great effort it took to not only carve out this estate from the wild, but to maintain it against nature's tendency to creep back and erase the mark of human existence.

Caleb could only guess at what things he might find in the rolling hills covered with woods that surrounded him. He could hardly imagine what it would be like to disappear into their gentle folds and crawl on his hands and knees so that he would not miss any detail. He glanced at Sara, and she stared back through the windshield, frozen with anticipation. Caleb could barely wait to see how she moved when she was released to follow the fragrant breeze.

Caleb stood on the grand porch. For a moment he sat in one of the wooden rocking chairs and stared out over the grass and water. In all of this space, he thought, he was alone. In a world where people seemed to be crawling on top of one another, clawing and screaming at each other, he had found a succulent piece of quiet. He rocked, listening to the chair creak as his weight settled into it. Even that gentle sound seemed loud, rubbing hot against the silence.

He stood on the tips of his toes while he felt for the key on top of the molding above the doorway where Frazier said his father always kept it. Tumblers fell into place and the oak door with a lion's head knocker swung open with only a muffled creak. The air was stale and still. When

he stepped into the hollow darkness, he shivered in the presence of so
many ghosts from the past he was sure were waiting for him.

Caleb found himself in a portion of the house clearly meant to impress a visitor with the owner's wealth and power in an age when homes
were not merely places to rest, but were the hubs of business, entertain-
ment and gentlemanly pursuits.

The ceiling in the circular room had to be at least twenty-five feet
high, and it opened up to a second floor landing connected to the ground
floor by a spiral staircase. Its ornate spindles and steps twisted so subtly and naturally that it seemed to cascade to the floor like a waterfall.
A chandelier with hundreds of tiny, dangling crystals dominated the
room. Under his feet, a white marble floor glistened in the dusty shafts
of light that managed to penetrate tiny gaps in drawn velvet curtains.
When his pupils finally adjusted, Caleb could make out life-size portraits lining the walls and glowing in the dirty light. Under each, a tall
ceramic urn that probably contained the ashes of the person immortal-
ized by the artist rested on a small table.

Their eyes followed him. Their lips seemed to move and their dead
breath polluted the air. Caleb gasped and stepped back toward the door.
He found the light switch and the chandelier flickered, blinding him for
a moment. He rubbed his eyes. He was astonished that he could have
been spooked by what were nothing more than pieces of fabric and
paint.

Caleb recognized the square face and stern, almost angry expression
of the man in the largest painting. The town's founder, Marcus McCoy,
posed wearing a drab, dark nineteenth century suit and tie and sitting
in a heavy wooden armchair. His hands were tense, gripping the ends
of the chair arms so tightly that the painter managed to capture his taut
tendons. His black hair was slicked back over his head. Caleb could
see a vague resemblance to Frazier in the elongated shape of his face.
But that was where the similarities ended. This man's wild blue eyes
revealed an almost soldier-like intensity and resolve. It was as if the
very object of his desire was dangling in front of him just out of reach,

and he was prepared to crush anything to get at it. If anybody could have convinced people to follow him into the unknown, it was Marcus McCoy.

The portraits of his descendants depicted men who seemed only lazy and bored, even smug at times. Their postures were less rigid, their bodies softer, their eyes dull and cloudy, their expressions devoid of purpose. Even their hands seemed tender and frail. Clearly they had enjoyed the wealth and luxury afforded them by their patriarch's labor. They seemed to grow more debauched and weak by the generation, that is until Maximillion McCoy came along. His portrait was the most recent. Perhaps in his late fifties, he posed wearing a blue three-piece suit, sitting in the same heavy armchair as Marcus McCoy. With the exception of a bushy mustache and his clothes, he could have been Marcus McCoy. The same intensity shot out of his blue eyes like daggers, daring anyone to question him. His stern expression evidenced a man hardened by some adversity, a man who would not compromise. Caleb reared his head back in disbelief when he realized that this man must be Frazier's father.

Caleb walked down the hall to the left of the foyer. He found himself in the dining room, which smelled of old wool and furniture polish. The walls were lined with gold leaf wallpaper on which mythical creatures were forever captured in the naked poses of love and death. In one scene, an armor-clad warrior raised his shield against a two-headed serpent, while in another a plump cherub took aim with his bow and arrow at a beautiful maiden napping underneath an olive tree. Caleb could picture nineteenth century guests bound up in stiff formal attire as they sat at the heavy mahogany table, noting the risqué theme with astonished breaths.

Across the hall in the kitchen, he was greeted by the fresh, delicious smells of roasted garlic and onions still lingering from a recent meal. In violation of the style and history of the house, stainless steel fixtures and cabinets replaced wood and glass. A refrigerator hummed softly. The space was hard, practical and functional, reminding him more of a bomb shelter than a kitchen. It was as if it was intentionally designed to ward off the casual presence of life so often found in the usually warm, friendly places where family meals are prepared.

He searched for a list of instructions that Frazier said would be on one of the counters. Caleb could find nothing. He opened several of the drawers under the counter but he could see only silverware and countless other utensils. In one drawer his hand felt the outline of a revolver behind a tray of fondue forks. Caleb withdrew his hand quickly as if the thing had bitten him. Although he was curious, Caleb was unfamiliar with guns, admittedly afraid of their potential for destruction.

Caleb sat down on a stool. He scratched his head while he glanced around the room. He decided he would just have to improvise if any emergency arose. The only thing he was really worried about was feeding the horses, but he could call a veterinarian if he could not figure it out for himself.

Caleb poked his head through a door in the rear of the kitchen. A plain oak staircase led to the second floor, its steps worn unevenly by busy feet over the generations. Caleb climbed the stairs, then moved down a long corridor that was dimly lit by small crystal sconces. He tried two of the doors, but they were locked. The third door opened. A dark wood canopy bed and matching nightstand occupied most of the room. A clock on the mantle ticked loudly. It was one hour slow. Although the room was neatly arranged, it was dusty from lack of use. But Caleb nevertheless felt more at ease there, where no human musk still lingered, where he was not intruding on anyone's privacy.

Before he went back to the car to retrieve his things, he made a quick tour of the rest of the home. The bathroom down the hall had been renovated with tiled floors and walls and a hot tub. The other unlocked doors on the second floor revealed two more spare bedrooms. They were a bit larger and exposed to more sunlight than the room he chose, but they each had narrow twin beds that promised to be confining and uncomfortable.

Downstairs, Caleb found a billiard room with a fully stocked bar and a library with shelves of books stacked to the ceiling, soft leather chairs and a marble fireplace. He opened a set of double pocket doors and beheld the ballroom. A mural had been painted on the walls, capturing the house and the grounds with a brilliant variety of natural colors, perpetually sparkling in the sun. His footsteps echoed off the hardwood floors. The sound triggered his imagination. For a moment, men and women all around him held each other at arm's length and twirled and smiled in the candlelight. The women's long dresses hid their feet, making them seem is if they glided effortlessly, held above the ground by their starched and stiff escorts. A quartet softly played the classics.

Caleb parted the heavy purple curtains and threw open the French doors at the opposite end of the ballroom. The doorway opened to a vast, marble veranda with a wrought iron railing in the shape of a vine and flowers. It afforded guests a sweeping view of the lawn behind the house and the forest beyond, where they could snatch a quiet moment away from the heat and activity.

Caleb leaned over the railing. A breeze carried the eye-watering sweetness of honeysuckle. He counted each of the rooms in the order he had discovered them. Not including closets and bathrooms, the house had fifty-two rooms. And in each one of them, if only for a second, he had felt that someone was close enough to pull on his sleeve.

Chapter 7

IT WAS TRUE; HE was not the stuff of old stale money, pampered from birth. He was a self-made man, and he was proud of that. With only five hundred dollars, he had pulled himself out of poverty to build a lucrative business hauling sludge and garbage from New York and New Jersey to places in Ohio that no person ever heard of. He had been unstoppable, finally selling it all to a corporation a year ago for some sixty million dollars. He did all of this, and he was only fifty four years old.

But none of that mattered here in Promise. To these pompous fools who fancied themselves to be the American equivalent of royalty, he was only a crass, foul-smelling barbarian, unfit to share their selfish existence. When he had tried to buy the house and the land, they fought him every step of the way, matching him dollar for dollar in a war fought by lawyers and engineers. But they won, and stopped him from tearing down the creaky, Victorian shack to make way for the home he had planned in his mind since he was a hungry child gazing across the railroad tracks to the wealthy neighborhoods. He did not like being denied, and he hated the sour feeling of defeat that ravaged his stomach like some disease.

"But Marcus Hearn is far from finished yet," he announced to himself as he surveyed the small complex of barns and outbuildings that once served to sustain the people who built the original house.

Certainly, he could not level the historic home, at least according to them and their convoluted laws, but no one ever said he could not destroy everything else, and build a home so large and sprawling that it would make the old house seem like a broken down tool shed in comparison.

He climbed into the seat of a used backhoe he had purchased for the momentous occasion, and started the powerful diesel engine. He smiled when he thought of the damage he was about to do, and wondered if anything could taste so sweet as this act of revenge and defiance he was about to undertake. He imagined that when he had finished the job, and was caked with the dust and debris of the stuff he had torn down, he would wash it off in the shower like so many of their insults, and smoke a cigarette as he watched trucks and materials rumble like thunder across the quiet countryside to build his dream home.

He forced the backhoe into gear and moved toward the largest, rickety barn first. When he was close enough, he stopped and engaged the massive arm and bucket. It was not just an extension of his own arm or will, but it felt like the very fist of God, swinging back and forth to right the injustice done to him by these selfish bastards.

With each stroke, wood was crushed and smashed to splinters, offering only the slightest resistance to the yellow painted piece of steel he was so adept at wielding. He quickly realized, though, that he was not doing enough damage. Although the death of the barn was so purely gratifying, he would be there for days, and his schedule for construction simply did not allow for any delays. He paused for a moment. He noticed that the structure already seemed to be leaning to one side. He thought if he could push it that way it might fall in one dusty, glorious heap he could piss on with impunity.

As gently as he could, he touched the broad side of the bucket to the side of the barn and then gradually increased the power. From somewhere inside, wood beams moaned, then finally cracked under the strain. Finally, the whole thing tumbled like a house of cards, crashing to the ground in a deafening roar that made him understand what a tornado or tidal wave must sound like as it swept across the land.

He shouted and hooted and threw up his arms in a display that surely would have offended any decent resident of Promise. He suddenly wished he had distributed flyers around town inviting every one of them to come and see what he thought about their precious conformity and heritage.

He began to scoop debris from the foundation of the barn using the teeth of the bucket. As the bucket lifted the broken pieces of wood and sections of the slate roof, he inadvertently dug up portions of the dirt floor the building had sheltered. On one pass, he failed to balance several planks of wood properly on the bucket, and they slid off to reveal the ancient black dirt he had disturbed. He first thought he saw a small chunk of concrete resting on top of the dirt pile, but when he focused on it for a moment he realized it was something else entirely.

He turned the engine off and approached it with a curious gaze, tilting his head to one side as if that might somehow afford him a better vantage point. He reached out to touch it, to be sure that the sweat that had run down into his eyes had not somehow distorted his vision. He pulled the hard white sphere from the blackness and knew, even before he saw the empty, lifeless eye sockets staring back, that he had uncovered a human skull. But before he could rationalize the existence of a single grave underneath the barn, he gazed around to find himself standing in a sea of bones, skulls and death that someone had tried to hide from the world. Before he walked back to the house, he counted some fifty bones and twenty skulls, most of which appeared to have been shattered or punctured by something. He was no scientist, but he knew that these people, whoever they were, had not died of old age.

The sheriff, Millstone, did not seem at all fazed by the news when Mark called him and told him what he found, but he was quiet for a long time. In fact, the only thing Mark remembered hearing him say was that he would be right out.

Mark smoked a cigarette on the porch while he waited for him.

He felt strange about calling him for help after they had exchanged harsh words in the past. When Mark first moved to this place, he found Millstone sitting in his car watching him from the road on several occasions, as if to warn him with his presence that he was not welcome, and that he would be watched in everything he did on his land. When Mark finally demanded to know what the sheriff wanted, he only said that he was doing his job, and that Mark should not raise his voice to him but should just mind his own business.

Mark had seen the worst of men in Vietnam, and he had killed a number of men himself there. He was not about to be intimidated by some Barney Fife with the intelligence of a donut.

When Mark saw the sheriff's car make its way up the driveway, he stood up and flicked his cigarette butt out into the yard. He walked out to greet him as the car stopped, determined not to become angry this time.

When Millstone stepped out of the car, he did not smile or wave or even speak. He did not even look at Mark; rather his eyes darted from side to side, and occasionally over his shoulder as if to check if anyone else was around.

"Sheriff," Mark said in his best hearty, country voice.

"Hearn," he responded, only grasping his hand for a split second before turning to look at the remains of the barn Mark toppled. "Out there?" he asked, and started walking over to the backhoe.

For the first time, Mark saw the sheriff out of his car and he noticed that he was a big man. Although he was probably about Mark's age, he stood at least six feet two and weighed two hundred pounds. He was broad shouldered and walked with the gait of a man who was used to getting his way in this beautiful, out of the way place. Cowboy boots, jeans, a brown uniform shirt and stiff wide-brimmed hat completed the picture of this local dictator. Mark glanced at his side and immediately identified a Colt forty-five-caliber pistol that hung there, the ultimate threat of force that made Mark wonder if he held it front of the mirror at night and likened himself to Clint Eastwood.

Millstone stopped suddenly and turned his head to one side, revealing sharp features in profile that gave him the look of a bird of prey that jerked and bobbed its head for a better view of a meal that might be scurrying across the ground below.

"What the hell are you doing out here anyway?" he demanded, without ever turning to face Mark.

"I'm just tearing down an old barn, Sheriff. There's no law that says I can't do that, is there?

"No, I guess not," he muttered.

Mark overtook him, arriving by the backhoe first to show him what he had found.

"You see Sheriff," Mark said while he picked up one of the dirty skulls, "this is only one of them, and they all have holes in them. Pretty strange, don't you think?"

Millstone grabbed the skull out of Mark's hand and held it up to the early afternoon sun. For a long moment he stared back into the black pits that once held eyes and color and life. It was almost as if he was looking at somebody he knew.

"Yeah, I guess it is pretty strange," Millstone whispered to himself as if he suddenly realized that everyone will look like that one day after rotting in the ground. He turned the skull to examine where part of the bone was shattered and had fallen away.

"They all look like this, huh?" he said when he turned to look into Mark's eyes for the first time since he arrived.

Mark stared back. He saw something in those dark eyes that he did not remember from his previous encounters with the sheriff. This time his eyes were focused and black, almost as if they were full of the moist dirt that had hidden the bones for so long. They trapped the light and gave no reflection of this man or what he was feeling. His eyes were dead to the world.

"Well, see for yourself. It looks like they were all killed the same way."

Millstone laughed.

"Is it murder now, Mr. Hearn?"

Mark could feel his temper rise to the top of his throat and he gritted his teeth against the urge to growl and hurl insults.

Mark Hearn was a man who was used to being taken seriously, and nothing infuriated him more than when he thought his opinion was being brushed aside like a child's nonsensical prattlings.

"This is nothing to laugh at, Sheriff. How and why do you think all these bones got here? The wind certainly didn't blow them across my field into my barn."

Millstone tossed the skull into the rubble and walked back toward the house.

"This is some old land out here Hearn, who knows what went on back then. It could be a family plot, or maybe it's an old Indian cemetery. They didn't use no tombstones, you know what I mean?"

"So what are you saying, you're not going to do anything about it?"

"What the hell do you want me to do about it, write the President of the United States about some old bones?"

"Well you could at least call the state police; they might bring some people out here."

Millstone stopped in his tracks. Obviously, the idea of bringing outsiders into this situation did not sit well with the sheriff. Mark hurried to catch up with him.

"Alright," Millstone said while he shook his head to show that he agreed only with great reluctance. "I'll get some people out here, there's no need to call the state dicks. All they do is grunt and stumble through the weeds like a bunch of drunken teenagers."

Realizing that he was now in the position to dictate terms to one of these small town cronies, Mark was going to apply pressure simply to watch the man squirm, if for no other purpose.

"I don't know, Sheriff. I think we need the resources of the state police, I really do."

Millstone's face was more crimson than a tomato. He pointed his finger at Mark and tapped in the air to emphasize every syllable of the words he spoke.

"Well, I'm not calling anybody I don't know, and that is that. Do you understand me, Hearn?"

"Oh, I understand now. But don't worry, you don't have to call anybody...I will."

Millstone took a step back and smiled calmly and warmly, as if he was one of Mark's best friends.

"That would be a mistake, a serious mistake. Why don't you just leave it up to me and let me do my job."

Mark now knew that broad smile was a practice intended to hide such veiled threats when in the company of others. The sheriff was accustomed to harassing the hitchhikers and other poor, ugly travelers who happened across his path. It was clear that this man was not just a petty, unfulfilled authority figure without the guts to act on his intent. But he was messing with the wrong man this time, a man who would not back down from the fight.

Mark took a step toward him and stared back into those hard eyes and tense face.

"Forget it, Sheriff. I'm going to walk back to my house, go into the kitchen and pick up the phone. Then I'm going to call the state police and the newspapers and have them crawl up your ass. Remember, not you or anybody else in this shitty, godforsaken place is going to tell me what to do."

Mark walked away before Millstone could muster any type of response. He smiled to himself as he climbed the stairs to the porch, but wondered if he was really prepared to do everything he promised. But that was not the point anyway, he reminded himself. It was all about power, and Mark knew that he could always pull rank over a fool like Millstone.

"Alright, hold still, Hearn," Millstone commanded.

Mark stopped just as he reached the front door.

"What are you going to do Sheriff, arrest me?" he taunted, without even turning to face him.

"No, I want you to stand in one place so I can kill you."

Mark whirled around and found himself staring down the barrel of the big forty-five. Millstone was smiling again, mocking him, preparing to issue the last word in this duel. Mark knew at that moment that he was utterly alone, and could do nothing to stop him from pulling the trigger and setting off a chain reaction of explosions that would cause a piece of metal to bury itself in his body.

For the first time since Vietnam, Mark was so completely frightened that in a slow motion blink of his eyes, he saw through the haze of his own selfishness and self pity, and understood those wonderful things he had lost somewhere along the way. There was Molly, his beautiful and fragile ex-wife, whom he had completely shut out of his life until she was nothing but a quivering shell of herself, and had no choice but to leave him. His brother, too, he had left behind because he felt that he only wanted to suckle the tit of Mark's success, otherwise too lazy to forge an existence of his own. Then he pictured the countless, nameless faces of people he had known only for a moment, but had ignored, insulted and disregarded, only because he never felt truly deserving of any love, affection or attention from any of them.

While his eyes were closed in that pause that marked the halfway point of his last blink, Mark shed the storm of tears he stored away for so long. He felt as if his soul was melting and draining to his feet to form a black, steaming pool of ooze. But also in that fleeting yet eternal fraction of a second, he forgave himself and hoped that someday they might all see him differently as well. Before he had opened his eyes for the final time, he decided that he would not beg. The least he could do was die as a man, like all the Marines he watched fall into the soft, bloody mud without even permitting a whimper of regret to escape their lips.

"Semper fi," he whispered as he heard the terrible end of his world and simultaneously felt the searing piece of metal punch him in the skull.

Just before everything went black, while Mark's brain attempted in vain to reroute some of its life-giving functions to pieces of its matter that had not been splattered on the door behind him, Mark stared into the deep blue sky.

***

Sheriff Millstone holstered his gun only when he was sure the annoying, whining troublemaker was dead. Although he knew from the tremendous damage he had done that the wound was certainly fatal, force of habit made him wait to be sure the body twitched and gasped and was finally still before he went about disposing of it. More than once he had been sure that he had killed a man, only to contend with him rising up suddenly out of unconsciousness screaming for mercy, splattering blood on his uniform during the struggle. He discovered that bloodstains were difficult to remove from his clothing, and he took great care to avoid the effort.

He dragged Mark Hearn's body by its feet into the house and dropped him on the floor just in front of the open door. He retrieved a canister of gasoline he stored in his car, and dumped it on the couch, chairs and table in the living room and dining room.

Just as he lit a match, he glanced around at the fine woodwork above the doorways and the tall windows that gave one an endless view of the wilderness. He thought it was a shame to destroy such a fine piece of his ancestry just to burn one body. But he did as he was told; every one of them must look like an accident that could at least be logically explained. There must be no sudden disappearances to arouse the suspicion of relatives and other outsiders who might care to make a name for themselves.

"Yes!" he exclaimed when the flames began to lick at the walls and ceiling.

He felt the searing heat on his face, the smoke stinging his nostrils and throat. He began to cough, but he could not force himself to leave the house. He loved to watch the cleansing, sterilizing flames at work. It was sheer power. When his eyes watered so profusely that he could no longer see, he stumbled out of the doorway.

It was a good way to hide what he had done, to hide the truth about this man and this town. After all, he would be the one to investigate the charred remains, and would of course find in his report that smoking in bed was the cause of the terrible blaze.

As he walked back to his car, he wondered for a moment why he did not feel guilty or saddened about killing another human being. He tried to find some voice inside his head to remind him that murder was wrong and punishable by death, but he could feel nothing. He enforced the law in Promise, and the law was whatever kept everybody happy and secure, locked away with each other like always.

Chapter 8

CALEB HAD CHANGED INTO jeans, a pair of Merrill hiking boots and a dingy T-shirt worn paper-thin by years of washing. He stood on the cavernous front porch of the mansion that was, at least temporarily, his. His eyes swept across the vast land that was going to be his wonderful playground.

He walked to the Stingray and opened the door. Sara leaped out, but immediately sat down in front of him. He was amazed that her bond to him was so strong as to prevent her from running in this expanse without his permission. Perhaps, he thought, she was so over-stimulated by the strange environment that she was confused and frightened, clinging to him for security.

He stroked the top of her head and she wagged her tail. Then he stood back.

"Go on...go play."

Still, she remained at his feet, her eyes fixed on him.

Caleb started to walk across the driveway toward the lake. Sara followed in his footsteps, crouched and alert, her muzzle tilted up to catch the scents carried on the gentle wind.

As they reached the manicured lawn that sloped down to the lake, Sara caught site of a stately robin poking and prodding the grass for food about twenty five yards away. Keeping low to the ground to minimize her profile, Sara stalked the bird, moving ahead of Caleb quickly. When she got within only few feet of the robin, it could tolerate her presence no longer. Its wings flickered as it took flight over the water. Even though Sara had failed to capture her intended prey, she had discovered her natural ability to hunt. As if to celebrate this milestone, she followed the bird from the ground at blinding speed then pranced confidently when she lost sight of the beating wings, content at least to have driven it off.

When Caleb caught up with her at the pebbly shore of the lake, she was lapping up water and shaking her tail wildly with excitement. Suddenly, her ears pricked up and she wrinkled her wet nose to better analyze the microscopic particles of another plant or animal that floated about the air and aroused her curiosity.

She quickly turned her head back toward the house and Caleb followed her gaze to a portly, gray groundhog casually basking in the sun. As if she could know what a slow, lazy beast it was, Sara charged it at full steam. She seemed to glide across the uneven ground. Caleb could see the muscles in her hindquarters flex and release each time she pushed off her back legs. When the groundhog finally realized it was being pursued, it tried to move away, but it had neither the quickness nor the cleverness to escape. Sara caught it from behind. Like some big African cat, she swiped at its hind legs with one of her paws, sending it tumbling through the grass.

However, catching the hog was one thing, deciding what to do with it was completely another. As it got back to its feet, Sara only stared at it curiously and wagged her tail, then looked back at Caleb as if to ask his advice. At first, the large rodent took on a defensive stance. But when it realized it would not be immediately attacked, it went on the offensive, apparently understanding Sara's hesitation as sign of weakness. It grunted aggressively, then dragged itself across the grass and threw itself at her. Sara stepped to the side, avoiding the clumsy attack. Though she was nimble enough to escape injury by the beast, Sara became concerned by its repeated attempts to do battle, and she trotted back to Caleb, occasionally glancing behind her to be sure she was not followed.

Caleb looked out across the silver, sparkling surface of the lake. Near the shore, fluffy cattails flexed collectively in the perfumed wind. He bent down and found a smooth stone, shaped like a silver dollar. He rotated it between his thumb and forefinger until he found a secure grip, and then hurled it out across the water, sending it skipping across the surface. Each time the stone touched the water, perfect circles of waves radiated out from the point of impact, disrupting the glassy calm.

Alerted by the sudden movement, Sara leaped into the blue water to follow the stone. Although she had never swum before, with the exception of only a few floundering strokes, she immediately began to paddle gracefully as if she had been born into the sea. When she could not find anything floating on the surface, she emerged from the water and shook off the excess, then waited with tense muscles, ready to undertake the vain effort again. Caleb obliged and sent the next stone sailing far out into the lake. Once more, Sara hurled herself into the water.

Caleb sat down on a patch of grass and was instantly struck by the silence and calm, as if he had been tapped on the head by a sledgehammer. There were no cars and no echo of music or conversation, not even the vague distant hum of electrical equipment. There was only the soft, high pitched ringing in his ears.

In the vacuum created by the absence of man-made distractions, Caleb began to understand what it must have been like to have been alive when the very sky was one's shelter, the ground served as a bed and the trees were the only walls to speak of. He thought about the wind, the water that gently responded to it, and the plants all around him that sprouted toward the sun. He tried to pinpoint the location of various animals he heard scurrying, jumping and slithering through the brush. Sometimes the only sign of the presence of these small creatures was a swaying blade of grass or a muted rustle. It was truly a complicated web of existence, each living thing depending on another to be either its predator or its prey. He could feel his existence now in the real sense, not in some existential realm where he was the center of the universe. He was nothing here in this place except for one more source of heat that was just as expendable as the smallest worm.

He and Sara walked around the lake, skirting the mysterious forest until they found a narrow dirt path that wound through the trees out of sight, obscured by shafts of light penetrating the canopy and colliding with the shadows. Caleb took a breath and stepped into the labyrinth.

Until his eyes adjusted to the pale light, he had to feel his way along the damp, moss-covered trunk of a tree that had to be at least twice as thick as Caleb's body. When he could see, he found himself in a place where he felt, oddly, safe and whole.

A bed of fallen pine needles provided a soft carpet cushioning each of his steps, as if he were walking on a cloud. The wind only managed to find its way into the forest in occasional, short-lived gusts, lacking enough force to disturb the damp stillness.

All around him, different species of pine, oak, maple and birch trees stood at attention, as if only a fraction of second before they had been mingling and moving among each other like soldiers at ease. He pushed all his weight against one of them, just to measure its incredible mass and strength.

A sense of well-being swept over him, releasing what seemed like years of knotted tension in his mind and muscles. For a dizzying moment, he thought he might collapse in a formless, slobbering blob.

Sara ran by him on the path, then stopped, scanning for anything that might run from her, offering the opportunity for a thrill. She lowered her head and lifted one of her front legs. Caleb realized that Sara was pointing at something, displaying the traditional pose of a hunting dog without ever having had the benefit of an example.

In the distance, Caleb heard several muffled snorts. Were it not for the nervous flick of its white tail, he would never have been able to distinguish the camouflaged body of the deer that had paused to study him. And Sara had found it too. As Caleb instinctively reached out to grab her collar, she began to chase it.

Immediately, the deer turned and ran. Caleb could see its white tail rise and fall as it bobbed and weaved effortlessly through the maze of immovable trees. Sara was not far behind. She leaped several feet in the air to clear fallen logs and bushes. Whatever she could not jump over, she was small enough to slither under. She seemed to have radar, narrowly avoiding a fatal impact with a tree at the last second with a graceful and calculated change of direction. When she finally realized she had met her match, she grudgingly broke off the chase. Once more, she proudly trotted back to him, apparently finding a way to declare herself the victor in her own mind.

Caleb continued to follow the trail, its direction changing suddenly and sharply at various points for no obvious reason. If there was a local folk tale that explained this, he thought, it would probably involve a man driven mad by the betrayal of the beautiful woman he loved. No doubt this man shed his clothes in a jealous fury, vowing to live among the trees forever, because he knew they would never leave him. Caleb imagined that this man howled at the moon and danced through the forest night after night, wearing a path as random as the direction of his insane thoughts. If such a story were told, it would conclude with a warning to children not to play here because they might get lost and come upon the ghost of the scorned lover, who could still be heard howling on nights when the moon was bright and full.

After he passed through a thick grove of laurels, Caleb found his way blocked by a massive maple trunk that had toppled to the ground. He scanned its length and could see its dirty, exposed roots. He could not help but wonder what force of nature could have torn it from the ground.

While he contemplated whether or not he should attempt to climb over the obstacle or make his way through the brush around it, Sara leaped onto it, just shy of the top, then scaled it and disappeared over the other side. Not to be outdone by her stubborn determination, Caleb reached over the log with both arms, pulled himself up as far as his precarious grip on the slippery bark would permit, then managed to swing one of his legs over the top.

He sat there for a moment, stunned by what lay before him. A narrow stream ran down over smooth stones through a gully it had carved into the forest floor. It gathered in a deep, clear pool where rectangular slabs of stone formed a V shaped wall against the current. When the water backed up against the natural dam, it spilled over the top, creating a small waterfall on the other side, where it gathered at the bottom and continued on its path. On either side of the stream, birch and pine trees rose from its bank and leaned out over the water in sharp angles, defying gravity.

Sara quickly found the pool and slid into it, swimming and lapping up the water at the same time to satisfy her thirst. The clean cold water seemed to call him, to invite him to find what he had lost when he had grown up.

Caleb sat down on the bank, removed his shoes, then quickly peeled off his clothes. He stood there for a moment, completely exposed, sensing his surroundings with every part of his body. He placed one foot in, letting himself adjust to the temperature of the water that had not so long ago been ice and snow. He shuddered as his skin erupted into goose bumps, but he kept moving into the quiet pool. When he was in up to his belly button, he dropped down, immersing himself completely.

He felt as if he had been turned inside out and every one of his organs was dangling outside him in the water, floating and throbbing with pain. But his scream amounted to nothing more than some bubbles of air that found their way to the surface. After a few seconds, his heart began to pump again and he relaxed. He raised his head above the surface long enough to fill his lungs, and then he plunged down again.

When he opened his eyes, he could see the smooth stone, illuminated by rays of light making their way to the bottom in miniature beams. He listened to the trickle of the water as it entered the pool, and he watched it churning and foaming.

Caleb pretended that he had died, fallen in this watery grave, and he went limp, allowing his body to slowly float to the surface where it bobbed in the current, partially submerged. He wondered if his real death would be similar, if he would feel like he was floating toward the light.

When his lungs began to sting, he raised his head and gasped loudly, this time imagining that he was born for the first time, clean and new and sparkling. When he opened his eyes to the world, prepared to see it all as a new man, Sara smothered him. Caleb laughed while he staved off her frantic effort to lick him, and he played with her for several minutes this way, splashing and laughing, having forgotten everything else. Then, while Sara slept nearby on a bed of dry leaves, he soaked in the pool quietly, staring at the sky until he felt his stomach rumble with hunger.

After he dressed, Caleb decided to continue on the path instead of turning back, believing that it would eventually bring him back some-where near the house. However, after about an hour, he began to tire, slowing to a casual walk punctuated by intermittent stops to rest and catch his bearings. Sara too had lost her steam, diverting from the trail less and less. Just as Caleb began to question his decision not to turn back, he stumbled onto a grass-covered clearing surrounded by a curi-ously neglected wooden post-and-beam fence.

The fence had collapsed in many places, and only patches of its white paint remained. Even more strange was the fact that the field was not entirely flat, but gradually rose up on all sides to form a large mound in the middle.

Caleb stepped over one of the fallen beams and walked to the top of the mound. His attention was instantly drawn to the largest tree he had seen yet. On the other side of the clearing, a red oak tree towered over everything else around, in stark contrast to the uniformly green forest. Caleb walked toward it, drawn to its magnificence.

When he stood in the cold shadow it cast across the field, he caught a chill and began to shiver. He reached up and plucked one of the leaves from the lowest branch and examined it in the last of the day's sunlight. Translucent, it glowed a blood red, criss-crossed by veins that nourished it and disposed of its waste. It seemed to pulsate like human flesh. He released the leaf and watched it fall to the ground.

Near him, one of the tree's massive limbs had fallen and pierced the mound, acting as a spear. The force of the impact had overturned some dirt that was still dark, not yet bleached by the sun. He glanced up to a hole in the cover of the tree's leaves marking the place the limb had been ripped from, violently it seemed, and certainly recently.

Sara sniffed at the fresh dirt on the mound. With loud grunts, she sucked in some intriguing scent buried beneath the surface. She began to dig a hole, throwing dirt high into the air. Caleb scolded her. Sara stared at him, her muzzle stained with the moist, black soil. She went back to digging.

"Sara, stop it!" he screamed.

She kept attacking the hole as if her life depended on it. Caleb finally grabbed her by the collar and dragged her away.

They soon passed the gray barn he had seen from the driveway when he first arrived. The horses grazed in their pasture, still indifferent to him. Sara was intimidated by their size, swinging wide of them on her way past. Relieved that he had found his way back, he could think of little else but a hot shower, some food and an ice-cold beer.

He bounded up the stairs to the front door, but paused in the round foyer of the old house, greeted by the portraits and stale smell of history that made him wonder how many people before him had stood there. He studied the face of the old man in the heavy chair and he thought about opening the urn for a brief moment, out of a morbid impulse to see if any teeth or bones had survived the cremation.

Chapter 9

CALEB FOUND A SIX-PACK of beer in the refrigerator, then fried a hamburger and topped it with cheese, tomatoes, onions and mayonnaise. He took his meal out to the front porch, sat down on the top step and ate and drank beer while the sun set, giving center stage to the night. When the glow of the day finally faded, he was reminded why people used to fear the darkness.

Without glaring, electric light, the night was like an inky black sheet draped over the land. The moon too seemed shut out by the darkness, reduced to a hazy sliver that struggled to glow in the distance. The stars, however, were the highlight of the evening. The absence of any other sources of light permitted them to shine like candles in a dark room, beacons of life. Their pulsating, billion year old beams cut across almost immeasurable distances to find this planet. Caleb knew that some of the shimmering, miniature streaks were only phantoms because their sources had long ago collapsed upon themselves, now black holes.

Sara sat up and growled at something in the dark. Caleb squinted to find what alerted her. He could make out some amorphous shapes, more like ripples in the sea of black really, moving smoothly across the grassy field. Caleb guessed they were deer feeding under cover of the night.

Caleb settled in a rocking chair. He closed his eyes and listened to the sound of the world that rose up only when the sun went down. Bats chirped as they used their radar to track down insect prey. Cicadas sung in waves welling up all around him, culminating in a deafening crescendo, then trailing off. Between these cycles Caleb detected dozens of other unidentifiable clicks, taps, whines and muffled cries, mixing and mingling with each other to form the chorus of the night.

In the arms of a warm breeze, his dog asleep at his side, he leaned his head back against the chair and wondered about everything. His mind expanded, filling every crevice in the sky.

Sometimes he was a boy, sometimes he was a man. Most of the time, though, he drifted somewhere between the two. He dressed in wool suits with sharp creases and swaggered confidently into his office every day, but he always blushed when a woman stared at him too long, wishing he could hide in the tree house he had built between two locust trees in his back yard when he was young. The adult world sometimes seemed so distant and boring. Caleb often found himself fascinated by the simplest things; a spider web, a puddle or his dog's long, velvety ears.

Ironically, it seemed that the boyish quality Caleb feared would be his undoing proved attractive to others. Women often liked him. To them, he was genuine and vulnerable. Even when they left him because he lost interest in going to cocktail parties or foreign movies, they cried and kept calling him for days to be sure he was all right. Men too seemed to tolerate him longer than they should. When he was lost and inattentive, his boss just nodded politely and let him alone, when he would have fired off a nasty memo to anyone else.

Caleb could not help but realize that any charm he possessed was only a crutch. He could afford to be only mediocre, ambiguous and undefined because he had a way of unwittingly endearing himself to others. A feeling of melancholy suddenly swept over him. As he often did, he vowed to himself that he would change, that he would be someone worthy of being remembered.

Caleb caught a pair of glowing eyes. He leaned forward. The tiny points of light stopped and stared back. He stood slowly, then the eyes bounced away, close to the ground. Caleb made out a small, stealthy profile as it darted to the cover of a shadow. Maybe it was a cat or fox. Maybe, he thought, one of the invisible ghosts he sensed everywhere had decided to take a form. Perhaps it was a sign meant for him, one he could not understand because his kind had long ago lost touch with its sense of the magical.

He opened another bottle of beer. Slowly he rocked and creaked with the rhythm of the night. He smelled dirt and wet leaves and his thoughts drifted back to the land. What did the plaque say, he built an agricultural empire? He could picture Marcus McCoy striding the length of his veranda while he inspected work in the fields with a telescoping monocular and barked out orders. At the fall harvest, there would have been wagons stacked with hay, corn and wheat, all of it needed for the war effort. Marcus McCoy would surely have smiled as his raw goods moved onto mills and other farms while gold filled his pockets in return. He tried to imagine the wrinkled, leathery faces of the people he would have needed for the back-breaking manual labor. They no doubt passed into obscurity, dissolving quietly into the dirt they tended. Maybe it was their invisible spirits he sensed at work around him.

Then it struck him; he had seen no evidence of farming or agriculture in Promise. The open spaces were either devoted to lawns or pasture. There were no silos or old rusting pieces of equipment. He had not even seen a broken-down stone fencerow. It was all very strange, he thought.

But Caleb quickly found himself nodding off, struggling to form a coherent thought. The mystery would have to wait until another day. He yawned, Sara stood. Caleb staggered inside and barely undressed before he fell on the bed, silent and unconscious. Sara quickly followed, curled at his head.

Despite the breeze and the quiet sky, his dreams were tortured, painful visions. They began as he stood looking up into the dark recesses of the red oak tree he had seen by the field. The branches were rough, gnarled and hairy, like thousands of arms and legs suddenly frozen in the motion of frantic death throes. The crimson leaves sprouting from the branches were plump and pulsating. The gritty, metallic smell of blood hung like a fog about the tree, filling his nose with the rancid smell of a slaughter.

Slowly, he stepped back from the tree, watching for movement, alert and suspicious. He panicked, and turned and ran, heaving for breath until he thought his lungs would explode.

When he thought he was far away, he summoned the courage to glance over his shoulder only to find that he was exactly where he had been, standing beneath the death tree.

Mad with fear, he dropped to his knees and waited to be consumed. The branches sprang to life and swooped down, grasping him with their cold fingers. Screaming, he was drawn up into the void and twisted to form the shape of his captors. White shafts burst through his skin, then unfurled. He could see his skin grow dry and brown as his blood was drawn up into the crimson leaves. His eyes grew dim and he was blind, his soul forever trapped in the wood, silent and in agony.

Chapter 10

T RINITY WOKE UP TO the sound of her mother hacking as she always did in the morning. She rubbed her eyes. Her mother popped her head into the room.

"They'll be here any minute girl, you better be ready," she warned with a growl, a lit cigarette dangling from her lips.

Trinity rolled over toward the small window just above her bed that afforded her a view behind the trailers to the forest. Out there was a world, she thought, with oceans and mountains and animals of all different sorts. Although she had not been to school in a long time, she looked at pictures in the magazines in the houses she cleaned, teaching herself to read enough to understand that there was so much she did not know.

She sighed while she dragged herself to the end of the bed and strapped her plastic leg to the chafed stub. They did not care whether it was comfortable or looked real, all they cared about was whether she could walk well enough to do her job. Some days it took all her will just to stand, let alone bend, reach or mop floors.

Trinity washed her face, then combed her long black hair in the mirror. She smiled to herself. She had been told she was pretty, like her grandmother. Maybe the man in the diner thought she was pretty too. Maybe he would take her away to some of those places she had read about, a beach with palm trees perhaps. But then she remembered the dead, empty space below her knee. She dropped the comb into the sink. Who could ever want her, she asked herself, limping and mangled as she was.

"Get your ass out here, I mean it," her mother scolded her. "I'm not gonna lose a week's pay again just 'cause of your laziness. I'll pass a whuppin' down the line to you the next time."

"Shut up," Trinity whispered.

Trinity put her hair back in a ponytail, pulled on her white uniform and made her way through "the camp" to where the buses would pick them up. The others were stirring too, stumbling out of their trailers, ready to face and hopefully survive another day.

Trinity waved to Mrs. Wellington, who was darning a sock while she sat on her front step and waited for her husband. Her gray hair was pulled back into a long ponytail. She squinted through half glasses at her work, fumbling with hands that were now twisted and broken from all the years of washing, scrubbing and mopping. She and her husband were among the oldest in the camp. Nearing seventy, the Wellingtons had been here for almost thirty years. Mrs. Wellington was like a grandmother to Trinity. She was always the calm voice when Trinity's mother was screaming, as she was often known to do. In a soft way, Mrs. Wellington would take her mother by the shoulder and remind her ever so gently that they did not have the luxury of outbursts or fits, seeing as they were always watched. And troublemakers never stayed for long.

Mrs. Wellington rushed over.

"Trinity, I made rhubarb pies last night. I saved one for you and your mother. You come by tonight and pick it up."

She smiled and pinched Trinity's cheek before she scurried back to her trailer. She opened the door and stuck her head inside.

"C'mon Allen," she screamed as loud as a whisper would allow, "you ain't never been late and I don't want to start today."

If there were a mayor of the camp, it would be Mr. and Mrs. Wellington together. They were experts at surviving, and moreover, they had figured out how to smile, kiss each other on the cheek and treat every day like it was their own, like they could stay home if they wanted and sit and swing on their porch. When new ones showed up, ragged and stunned, she and her husband took them cake or pie and told them about the place in which they found themselves. She would put the harsher, darker words to smiles or laughter to make them easier to swallow. After all, to come right out and tell people they were doing a life sentence might just make them crazy. She took her time, and did not leave until she was sure the new folks wouldn't kill themselves or run off.

Trinity glanced back. Mr. Wellington was on the porch in his overalls toting his lunch bucket. Trinity wondered how long he could keep working, as old as he was. And everybody wondered what would happen after that. Trinity's eyes welled with tears and she turned away. She knew they would be gone someday soon. No one who could not work ever stayed on long.

Trinity's mother caught up and they fell in with the others. There was Michael, who was about her age, with dirty brown hair and pale, blue eyes. He smiled wryly, looking her up and down. She stuck her tongue out at him. Then there were the Hispanics; Miguel, Angel and Fernando, and some new ones whose names she did not know yet. Some of them spoke English, and Trinity had learned a little Spanish, at least enough to know they were like everyone else, lost and most of the time hopeless.

In the distance, she could see a cloud of thick dust rising above the trees, moving closer. The buses were right on time. Just once she wished that they would be late, broken down somewhere, or better yet burning out of control.

Trinity and the others took their places in the single file line. Trinity recognized the bald head of Mr. Granger, a gardener, and she knew she was in the right spot. It would not do to be out of order. Everything had its place, they said.

Trinity's heart suddenly leaped into her throat. She dropped her coat and hobbled back toward the trailer as fast as she could. Some of the others in line reached out a hand to stop her, but she pushed them away.

She had forgotten about her dress, she had washed it in the sink the night before and it was still hanging on a limb outside her window. She glanced back over her shoulder. The buses were getting closer. If they saw the dress, they would take it. It was the only pretty thing she owned. She fell, then climbed back to her feet and snatched it off the branch. She stuffed it inside her uniform and made it back just as the buses stopped.

Her mother smacked her in the back of her head so hard that she saw a sudden burst of blinding light, then grabbed her by her ponytail and pulled her close.

"Quit fuckin' around, little girl."

Trinity winced, then pinched the loose skin under her mother's arm as hard as she could until she let go. By that time, it was their turn to climb on the bus. The driver examined her with longing eyes.

She took her assigned seat next to a window. The driver was counting heads in his rearview mirror. As the bus bounced along the rutted, dirt road she noticed some new faces. As always, their heads were hung low, their mouths slightly open, their eyes stunned and lifeless. They were still hoping it was all a dream.

Although Trinity was only fourteen when she came here, she remembered what it was like to be told that she and her mother would be here for a long time. She remembered what it was like to be robbed of lightheartedness and lazy days thinking about boys and dancing. But when she was alone in the dark, she got to thinking, planning a way across the river to the highway. She pictured that man's face again, and she prayed he would come back. She prayed that he would be the one to free her from her chains.

The sheriff's car slowly pulled alongside the bus as it entered town. He scanned their faces through the windows, threatening them, daring them to look back. Trinity hid her face too, leaning her head on her mother's shoulder. Her mother kissed her on the top of her head.

"I'm here baby," she whispered. "I'm here."

Chapter 11

CALEB SIPPED COFFEE WHILE the fog of sleep slowly cleared from his mind. Eventually, the image of the tree in his dream was nothing more than a vague, distant thought, soon to be evaporated completely by the glorious morning sunshine.

He found hay in the barn, and he filled the bins in each of the stalls with as much as they could hold. When each horse had its fill, he retrieved the rest for another meal. Caleb guessed that the horses were the best judges of how much they needed to eat. He watched them frolic, baiting each other and racing along the fence. Occasionally, they would let him reach out and rub their muzzles.

Without leaving his side, Sara lifted her nose to the wind to capture their scent. She whimpered when they galloped, anxious to join in the fray, but still too intimidated by their size and strength. Once, in a final, playful crescendo, the horses reared up on their hind legs, clashing hooves and chests in mock combat. Completely exhausted by their effort, they soon returned to grazing, occasionally swatting their tails at the flies that swarmed in the heat.

Caleb and Sara went back to the waterhole and swam, napped, and swam some more. Each time Caleb plunged into the water, he felt some piece of himself restored, his mind made clearer. As they made their way back to the house along the path, he realized he no longer cared about his job or the filthy city. He looked at the sun and decided that anywhere warmed by it was his home.

Caleb sat on the mound and stared at the giant red tree. Sara meanwhile found the hole she had started the day before and began to dig furiously. She pushed her nose deep into the dirt and began to bite and pull at something. Again Caleb had to drag her away.

After a shower and a meal of toast and scrambled eggs, Caleb and Sara climbed into the Stingray. It was early in the afternoon, leaving him plenty of time to pay Pete a visit. Caleb was hoping Pete might show him a good place to fish, somewhere with cool shade where he could lay back and do nothing at all if he wanted.

On his way through Promise, Caleb was once more fascinated by its surreal, movie-set quality. The sidewalks were clean and white. The grand houses were quiet. Judging by some grass clippings that had gathered in the street, their lawns had been cut recently, simultaneously it seemed.

In town, some people moved between their sleek cars and the stores. They walked slowly, casually, never once glancing at a watch or grimacing with the usual stresses of daily, hectic life. It was as if they had no particular place to go and they had all the time in the world to get there. Caleb stopped in front of the diner and strained his eyes to see inside. A man sitting at the counter sipped coffee while he read a newspaper. Trinity's mother was busy serving people at a table that was hidden from view.

Caleb pulled around the town circle. He could smell fresh mulch and dirt. Some pink and red carnations had just been planted around the statue of Marcus McCoy. Two women wearing sunglasses and gold watches sat on a bench and laughed quietly about something. A bell in the church steeple chimed one o'clock.

As soon as he was outside of town, Caleb pushed the car, accelerating through the turns, moving through all the gears on the straight-aways. Once, he slowed the car where skid marks on the blacktop led over a steep embankment down to the river. He pulled to the edge of the road, but the only evidence of any accident that remained was some broken tree limbs. He shook his head. Poor bastard, whoever it was.

When Caleb pulled into the dirt lot at the store, Pete was already waiting for him, holding the screen door open.

"I could hear that thing before I could even see you," he said while he pointed at the Stingray. "It makes a hell of a sweet rumble."

Caleb reached out and shook his hand.

"How are you doing, Pete?"

"The question is, how are you doing up there in that town? Run into the sheriff yet?"

Caleb laughed.

"Funny you should ask that, Pete. I think I saw him yesterday. I was in town, on the circle. I tried to back up and he was there, blocking my car. I'm not sure what he was doing, but he was talking on his radio. I think he was running my license plate."

Pete shook his head and stared at Caleb over the top of his glasses.

"I told you about the kind of man he is. At least you know enough not to trust him, to keep an eye on him."

Caleb nodded.

"And I will, believe me."

Pete walked behind the counter and bent down for something.

"I hope you came to fish, 'cause I don't feel like working any more today."

When he stood up, he had a fishing pole and a small tackle box.

Pete led Caleb back down to the whispering river. They walked along for about fifty feet and stopped where the water had washed out a portion of the shore, forming a calm, deep, black pool.

Pete bent over and pointed into the dark water.

"They hide here a lot of times, resting up. It's quiet and deep, they think they're safe down at the bottom."

Pete opened the tackle box and removed a white Styrofoam cup filled with dirt. He dug into it with his fingers and pulled out a writhing worm. He held it up to the light.

"Beautiful," he whispered, admiring it. "This batch of night crawlers I dug up in my yard are full of piss and vinegar."

In one calculated motion, Pete impaled the worm on a hook and cast it out into the water. He let it sink for a moment, then slowly reeled it in. Caleb squatted down to get a better look, but he could see only the murky blackness.

"What else do you know about Promise, Pete? I mean, did you ever hear any stories about it?"

"Except for that sheriff, I've never even really met anybody who lived there. But I have heard things second hand, nonsense from kids mostly. I also got a strange tale from Buddy Hoshburn, one of the old timers I used to golf with. He's dead now."

Pete glanced back and forth between Caleb and the line in the water.

"Why do you want to know?"

"Well, everybody's rich, everything is perfect. None of them seem to have a care in the world. That's not like any place I have ever seen."

Pete handed him the fishing pole.

"Now," he whispered as if the fish might be listening, "just let the worm dangle down there. Every so often just kind of move it up and down, make 'em think he's still alive and kicking."

Pete laid his apron on the ground and sat down on it. He cleared his throat.

"Buddy used to grow vegetables on a farm up the road, a bit closer to Promise. He told me that one day while he's sitting on his porch, he sees a man stumbling along out in his patch, steppin' all over the vegetables. He yells out, but the guy keeps wobblin' all over the place. He gets his shotgun, then goes out to shoo him away. Bud thought he was drunk or something. But when he gets there, he finds this guy, he's real thin and he smells. Bud saw that he had been shot in the leg, he was bleeding. Bud told me that he was laughing like he was delirious. Then I guess he said 'I just walked away', over and over again. Anyway, the guy collapses there in the field. Bud called for an ambulance, but Millstone comes instead. The sheriff tells him that he can get the guy to a hospital faster than an ambulance. Away he went. Bud never heard anything about the guy again."

"Did Bud ever call anybody to find out what happened?"

"I don't think so. I guess he didn't want to know anything else."

Caleb tugged on the pole several times, but nothing seemed to bite.

Pete leaned back and locked his hands behind his head, like a boy dreaming about what he was going to be when he grew up.

"The kids up at the overnight camps, they tell each other scary stories when they're sitting around the campfire. They say that Promise is full of vampires. They say that they snatch up little boys and girls who wander into the woods alone and keep them as slaves, feeding on them for their blood, that sort of thing."

Caleb laughed.

"Whatever they are they're not vampires. Maybe they're cold as fish, but not vampires."

The line jerked. Caleb held his breath.

"Nice and easy," Pete warned while he sat up, "you don't want to break the line."

Seconds later, a small brown fish was flapping on the ground; it seemed to be gasping for air.

"What do we do now?" Caleb blurted out between excited breaths.

"I don't keep 'em." Pete reached down and wrenched the hook from its mouth like he was pulling a cork from a bottle of wine, "I don't really like trout that much, I just like the thrill of the little game."

Gently, Pete submerged the fish in the water. They watched it dart away out of sight. Caleb leaned back on his elbows.

"I can't understand what they do for a living, I never see them going to or coming from any sort of job."

Pete pulled out two cans of beer from the tackle box and handed one to Caleb.

"I hope you don't mind, they're not cold."

Caleb opened the can and gulped down a mouthful of the beer. He didn't realize how thirsty he was. He finished it in a matter of seconds.

Pete smiled.

"I guess you don't mind so much."

Pete looked out across the water.

"I think it's old money up there, passed down over the generations."

Caleb nodded in agreement. He told Pete about the statue in the park, and about the portraits on the wall in the house.

Pete raised his eyebrows.

"Who would have ever thought that all those snobs came from a bunch of hardworking farmers? They probably sit on their asses all day long now, doin' that day trading, or whatever its called, with all that old money that got handed to them."

"Yeah, maybe," Caleb whispered to himself.

For the next half hour, they both sat silently, staring into the warm sky and listening to the muffled rush of the river that lulled them into a lazy summer trance.

Caleb thought about what Pete said, about the stories. Maybe they were just folk tales, a way of explaining things that people did not understand. But he could not deny that there was always a bit of truth in every lie, and he tried to draw a consistent theme that bound together the tall tales about this place. A wounded man who "just walked away" and images of vampires and slaves seemed more contradictory than consistent. One involved a shooting, a relatively common, mortal fate. The other concerned the walking dead, supernatural creatures that lived forever, drawing nutrition from human blood. Caleb closed his eyes. It was all foolishness.

Caleb let consciousness slip away and fell into a sleep filled with images of warm, passing shadows. He woke up after the sun disappeared over the mountains, leaving behind bright pink and orange streaks that seemed burned into the very fabric of the sky. Pete was gathering up the tackle box and fishing pole.

"I didn't want to wake you before, you looked like you needed the sleep."

"What time is it?" Caleb yawned.

"About eight o'clock."

"I've got to go." Caleb started to walk back toward the steps. "Thanks Pete, I'm going to run. I'll give you a call. I sure enjoyed the fishing."

Pete waved him off.

"Any time, I'm always looking for an excuse to get out. It's always more fun with somebody else."

Caleb drove slowly, tediously guiding the car through the curves. He could never have guessed how treacherous the winding roads proved to be in the dark, even when he was somewhat familiar with the sharp, banked turns.

Before bed, Caleb and Sara sat on the porch once more and basked in the sights and sounds of the night. The moon was clear and bright for the first time since he arrived, and it bathed the land in its white, eerie light. A howl in the distance broke the silence. Maybe it was a wolf or a coyote. The wail was not frightening though; rather it was sad and lonely, as if the animal were mourning a terrible loss. A gust of wind curled around his head, saturated with the smell of lavender and honey-suckle. It was all magic, he thought.

Chapter 12

WHILE THE SUN WAS burning just below the horizon, Caleb awoke, made some coffee and carried a cup of the steaming black liquid out to the barn. While he fed the horses and watched their muscles ripple under their glossy fur, he was reminded of the great amount of money and effort it took to care for them.

He thought there must be many horses in and around Promise, as keeping them is so often a hobby of the wealthy. But he could not imagine any one of the landowners here providing the physical labor to train, feed or maintain them.

"Of course." He slapped himself in the forehead. He suddenly remembered the crew of workers he had seen in the yard of the towering house in town. Caleb deduced that there must be a small community of workers living in broken down shacks, scratching out a living doing Promise's dirty work. And because they probably could not afford cars, they must live nearby. Surely Trinity and her mother lived there too. Caleb decided he had to find them. After all, who would know Promise better than the people who took out its garbage and swept its streets.

Caleb soon found himself crawling along Promise's perpetually quiet streets once more. This time though, he was scanning rear entrances and craning his neck to see behind fences, looking for a delivery truck or somebody in greasy overalls, any sign of reality.

He turned down a shaded, narrow alley. Around a corner, in the back of one of the old pristine white buildings, a single neon sign flickered, advertising that "Bud" was served within. Caleb smiled, pleased with himself. The town even let them have their own tiny watering hole. Caleb parked behind a rusted Ford pickup truck loaded down with hay.

When he pushed open the door, he was welcomed by the smell of overflowing ashtrays and stale beer. He stepped into the hot darkness. At first, he could only make out the twinkling multi-colored lights of a juke box tucked away in a corner and a couple of bare light bulbs suspended above a pool table. Gradually, he could distinguish the images of people, frozen in the motion of sipping a drink or chalking a pool cue, cautiously studying him. They had mistaken him, it seemed, for somebody else.

When they discovered he was not the person they had apparently feared, they began to move once more as if the door had never opened and the fresh air had never carried away the smoke that curled from cigarettes dangling from their lips.

Caleb found his way to the bar and sat down on a stool directly in front of a jar of pickled eggs. The label had turned yellow from the cigarette smoke and the grease that escaped from the small kitchen.

Behind the bar, there were bottles of cheap whiskey and tequila on plywood shelves, the favorites of those who identified with the hardship expressed in the worn-out country song whining from the jukebox behind him.

Caleb glanced along the length of the bar to the only other person seated there. He was wearing grimy coveralls and a stained baseball cap. He was sipping a beer, staring out into space. Caleb could see his eyes suddenly move, recognizing that he was being watched. He did not turn his head to meet Caleb's gaze, but instead looked sheepishly down into his beer and focused intently on it, as if it might reveal his future.

Over Caleb's shoulder, two Hispanic men played pool and talked to each other in Spanish. Each of them chuckled in response to the words of the other, and Caleb could not help but wonder if it was at his expense.

"What can I get ya?"

Caleb turned toward the sound of the hoarse voice and found an extremely large woman with gray hair pulled back in a long ponytail. She wiped her hands on a dirty apron while she waited for a response.

"A beer, Budweiser if you have it."

"That's what the sign says," she quipped sarcastically while she opened a cooler and retrieved a brown bottle.

She moved surely and deliberately, more like a man than a woman. The only feature, other than her hair, that established she was a woman and not some burly, gun-toting redneck were her breasts, which were disproportionately large even in comparison to her already enormous body. Each of them was the size of a watermelon.

She set the bottle in front of him and he reached for his wallet.

"How much do I owe you?"

"Buck."

Caleb gave her two dollars. Her face changed from a bitter mask to a wide smile accented by deep dimples at either end. She now beamed as if Caleb were an old friend she had not laid eyes on since high school.

"Any man who tips like that wants something," she giggled.

"No," Caleb smiled shyly, embarrassed because he had disguised himself so ineptly. "I used to work in this business, I know how important a tip is."

She leaned over the bar, revealing her generous bosom.

"I'm Lois and you're sweet, and you smell good," she whispered, glancing around to see if anyone else was listening. "If you come back later, I'll show you something."

Caleb nodded, indicating that he understood the nature of her invitation. Lois walked over to the other man at the bar, this time swaying her hips in an exaggerated way as she moved. She glanced back at Caleb and winked, then asked the man if he wanted anything.

"Whatever he wants, Lois, it's on me," Caleb offered.

The man turned and raised his head slightly so he could see Caleb from under the brim of his hat. He examined Caleb suspiciously for a moment, and then smiled.

"I'll have me a beer, Lois, and a whiskey shot."

The accent was southern, but it was very subtle, most of it probably lost after years of living in the North. Caleb moved down to the seat next to him and held out his hand.

"I'm Caleb."

"I'm Billy, Billy Montour."

He gripped his hand. Caleb could feel grease, grit and tough snake-like skin, the hallmark of a laborer.

"I'm not gonna ask why you bought me a drink. I guess I just don't care much. Besides, what does it matter, right? It's just a drink."

"Just being friendly, that's all."

Billy smiled again, revealing several missing teeth. The others were almost as brown as his eyes. Caleb guessed he was only about thirty-five, but the deep wrinkles in his thin face and the sad state of his dental work made him look as if he was fifty or even sixty.

Billy cocked his head and threw back the shot that Lois had placed in front him in one fluid motion. He closed his eyes for a moment, apparently relishing the experience.

He exhaled while he smacked his lips, demonstrating his satisfaction.

"Whoo boy, that is soooooo sweet!" He howled in a sort of curtailed rebel yell.

He opened his eyes. They seemed to have suddenly come to life. They were now a rich syrupy brown, wild with the promise of drunken mischief.

Caleb motioned for Lois who was standing nearby to pour Billy another. Caleb knew that the alcohol would soon numb Billy, who would then gladly reveal whatever he knew.

Billy swallowed the second shot as soon as his glass was full, then looked Caleb up and down with a shocked expression on his face.

"Well, judgin' by your looks, you sure don't work for a living. But I know y'all can't be one of them cause they'd never come in here."

This time, Billy motioned for Lois to pour him another drink.

"So, who the hell are you?" he asked before he threw back his third shot in the span of as many minutes.

"I'm up here watching the house of one of my friends who went away for a couple of weeks."

"Oh yeah, who's that?"

"Frazier McCoy."

The shocked expression returned to Billy's face. Lois leaned over the bar and whispered something in his ear.

"I appreciate the drinks and all, but I gotta get back."

Billy stood up, swaying slightly, tipped his hat to Lois and made his way toward the door. Lois disappeared into the kitchen.

Caleb dropped some money on the bar and followed Billy out the door, catching up with him as he opened the door of the hay-filled pick-up truck.

"What did I say?"

Billy placed his hands in front of him as if to stop Caleb from coming any closer. Then he thrust his hands in his pockets and spoke while he stared down at the ground and kicked the toe of his boot into the dirt.

"Look, I don't want no trouble. I know I shouldn't be drinkin' durin' the day, but I do my job and I don't bother anybody. Just tell Mr. Mc-Coy it won't happen again."

"I don't know what you're talking about. I don't even know the Mc-Coys very well. I'm from Philadelphia. I ran into Frazier McCoy a few days ago. He said he was going away and needed someone to watch his house."

Billy was quiet for a moment, then he flashed another toothless grin.

"Well, why in hell didn't you tell me that? I thought you were keeping an eye on me or something."

"No, I'm not going to tell anyone you were here."

"Alright then!" He howled. "Let's go on back in and have a couple more drinks!"

When they sat back down at the bar, Billy winked at Lois, who could only shake her head in disapproval.

"It's okay Lois, he don't even know the McCoys, he's just watching the house for 'em."

"I ain't saying nothing more, Billy. I warned you."

"I'm telling you Lois, it's all right."

Lois threw her hands up in the air and walked back into the kitchen. Although she appeared briefly several more times to pour more whiskey for Billy, she never looked at Caleb again or spoke another word.

When the alcohol replaced Billy's inhibitions he slurred forth an interesting story.

He grew up in a shack in Georgia. His father had no steady occupation except drinking, although he sometimes tended horses for meager wages at a nearby farm. He described his mother as "pregnant all the time," which condition denied him her attention, leaving him to find trouble instead.

By the time he was sixteen, he was an alcoholic who, like his father, made enough money grooming horses to buy a meal and some drinks. When he was twenty-one, he got caught stealing money from the cash register at a gas station. After spending two years in prison, he left Georgia, intending never to return. Since then he had drifted from one horse farm to another, working until he felt like moving on.

Billy came to Promise in response to an advertisement slipped under the door to his room. It read:

"Housing and Highest Wages Paid for Labor."

"So," Caleb asked, "is it true?"

"Well it seemed at first like it was. You see this is a real rich town and they pay us to do all the shit work. The town put up these trailers and cabins for us and every day they pick us up and take us to wherever in town we're needed."

"So how long have you been here?"

"Going on five years now."

"When are you leaving?"

Billy was quiet for a moment.

"I can't ever leave this place," he whispered.

"Why?"

"You wouldn't understand, you're not from here. You're an outsider. Matter of fact, I don't think the sheriff would like it much if he knew you were even here."

Caleb remembered what Pete told him.

"Millstone, he's the sheriff, right?"

Although Billy's eyes were only lazy slits, he opened them wide at the mention of the name.

"I'm drunk and I shouldn't be talking no more," he remarked, sounding more frightened than intoxicated.

"Listen Billy, I just want to know what's going on around here. Where are all the people, what do they do, why are they so wealthy?"

Billy quickly glanced around as if to see if anyone might be listening.

"You see," he whispered while he leaned over closer to Caleb, "there ain't no people in town, everybody lives just outside of it in these big mansions. But they keep all the buildings here real nice.

"What I can't figure is what any of 'em do for a livin'. They always seem to be home sippin' their drinks and havin' parties with the same old people all the time. Young and old, they never go anywhere. It's like the rest of the world don't exist at all."

Billy locked his fingers behind his head as if he were pondering one of the great mysteries of the universe.

"But they all got tons of money, money to burn. I don't know where they get it from, but they got tons of it."

He leaned forward and pounded a fist on the bar hard enough to shake their glasses.

"It ain't right that I work so hard and I got nothin' and they do nothin' but they got everything."

Caleb finished the rest of his beer in a single gulp. He was also feeling a wave of alcohol-induced courage.

"Just get the hell out of here then. Pack up your shit, then be gone before the next sunrise."

Billy shook his head violently back and forth.

"Better than me have tried. They leave, but no one ever hears from them again."

"What the hell are you talking about? What are you saying, that this place is like some black hole, that these people kill you if you try to get out?"

Billy shook his head again.

"I ain't ever seen no bodies, I'm just tellin' you that no one ever hears from them again. We're all just scared I guess, scared to find out if all the rumors are true."

"Why don't you just pick up the phone and call the cops or your family or the newspapers or something?"

Billy was now on the verge of tears. He wiped his nose on his filthy sleeve.

"Millstone is the only law around here, and he'd kill anybody who even looked at him wrong. We can't call anybody else cause they don't give us phones, they don't let us mail anything. We gotta buy what they sell to us, which is so expensive that we always owe 'em more. We ain't even allowed to have cars, even if we could afford 'em."

"What happens if you get hurt or sick? Tell the people at the hospital what's going on here."

"We gotta see their doctor. When people got to go to the hospital, we never see 'em again."

Caleb rubbed his eyes, expecting to wake up in his apartment in Philadelphia where things were familiar, simple and predictable. He could not believe that in the most populated state in the country there was a place where indentured servitude was still practiced.

Caleb closed his eyes. There had to be something he had missed, some circumstance that would logically reconcile Billy's story with this age of fast food restaurants and all night pharmacies.

"What about the McCoys, what do you know about them?"

"I know the old man is the head of the town council. Whatever he says around here goes. His family started this place I guess. Rumor is that his ancestors came up here along with a bunch of Negroes from somewhere down south."

Although he could still not piece together the consequences of time and history that had created whatever was going on in Promise, Caleb did not doubt Billy's desperate frustration and he felt terribly guilty for his life. He felt guilty because he had encouraged Billy to drink to intoxication. He felt guilty because he had choices and Billy had none. Most of all, he felt guilty because he had hope for the future, however slight, while Billy could only pray that he would live to get drunk another day.

Caleb thought about Trinity. He wondered if she even knew there was a dynamic, thriving world outside her invisible prison.

"You know where I am Billy. I'll be here for two weeks. If you want to get out of here, find me and you can go with me."

Billy buried his head in his hands.

"I ain't big enough to do that," he sobbed. "I'm just a drunk, like my daddy. I can hardly keep my hands steady enough to keep from pissin' all over the bathroom. I 'preciate your offer, but I'm six feet under already."

"Well, if you change your mind I'll be here for a while."

Billy nodded then stared out into space again.

Caleb left Billy exactly as he had found him, by all appearances completely unfazed by their conversation. Caleb, however, left with more questions than answers, but he could now see the grimy evil in Promise that was only sugarcoated by the fresh paint and picket fences.

Around every corner, the stillness and void of bustling activity reminded him that not only was this picture-perfect town actually dead, it was something worse. The community was only a neatly arranged storefront erected to deceive the world, to hide the suffering of others.

Chapter 13

B ILLY LOVED BEING DRUNK. It was pure religion in his mind, a frolic with God. In fact, the thousands of times he had been drunk marked the high points in his life. The sloppy state of mind hid him away from himself, and from the world. And Billy especially liked working when he was drunk.

He whistled a few bars of a song he had heard on the record player in the bar while he carried the bales of hay up the rickety ladder. He heaved them on top of one another, happily now.

Although he stumbled a few times, nearly toppling twenty feet to the barn floor, his lack of coordination was a small price to pay for the numbness. He was just relieved not to feel the throbbing arthritis in his hands and knees that seemed to grow worse each day.

Billy soon found himself thinking about the strange man who had bought him all the booze. Something he said really struck a nerve. So much so, that Billy occasionally paused from work to ponder his words.

Just pack up your shit and leave.

Billy counted the words, all seven of them. They just rolled off the stranger's tongue, as if what he asked was as simple as wiping his ass.

Billy laughed aloud at the idea. If he even tried, he would be signing his own death warrant. Like he told the guy, better men had run away and were never heard from again. Still, Billy wondered if there was not some way to do it. He wondered if there was still any rebel blood running through his veins. The question was, did he still have the guts, or had the alcohol robbed him of his soul just as it had stolen everything else he ever was, or would be.

While he hauled another bale up the ladder, he realized only that he was drunk, and that in the morning he would not even be able to think without taking another drink. In that condition, he was no match for the likes of the sheriff and his bunch. Still, maybe he would rather die trying to get away, even if there was nothing out in the world for him.

"What are you doin' Billy?"

Billy whirled around. He dropped the bale of hay, and it tumbled to the bottom of the ladder. Millstone was there, leaning against the barn door smoking a cigarette as if he had been there all the time.

He was a vision from hell, Billy decided. He was a mind-reading demon sent by the devil himself and it was all Billy could do to keep from pissing in his pants at the very sight of him.

"What's the matter Billy, cat got your tongue?"

"No, Sheriff, you just startled me that's all."

"Why did I startle you, Billy? What're you worried about?"

"Nothin', just I thought I was alone, that's all."

Millstone looked around while Billy stood frozen.

"You're runnin' behind. You got two more loads to deliver. What the hell have you been doin'?"

"Nothin'."

Millstone smiled, then he motioned for Billy to come down to where he was.

"C'mon, Billy. Come here."

Billy stiffly made his way down to the bottom of the stairs. Millstone leaned close and sniffed several times. His face screwed up with disgust.

"You've been drinkin' Billy, huh?'

"Well…yeah, I had a few at Pearly's."

"So I hear, Billy, so I hear. I also heard that someone was buying you drinks, a stranger, a young guy."

Billy started to sweat and shake.

"Yeah. I mean a guy bought me some shots, I never seen him before. I don't remember his name, but he told me he was stayin' at Mr. McCoy's place, while he was away I guess."

Millstone smiled again, pleased with himself.

"What did you talk about, the weather?"

"Naw, just jawing, that's all. I…I mean I didn't talk nothin' about us I mean."

Millstone poked his head outside the door.

"C'mon Billy," he said while he looked around outside, "I ain't worried about that. I know you wouldn't do nothing to upset the apple cart. I just want you to let me know when somebody's around that's all. I don't want to hear it from somebody else. When you don't call me, I get suspicious. You understand what I'm sayin'?"

Billy exhaled with relief.

"It won't happen again, Sheriff. I'll be the first to tell ya'."

Millstone pointed to the loft.

"Go on now, get back to work."

Billy nodded. He retrieved the fallen bale of hay and started back up the ladder.

Billy had no idea that anything was wrong, even when he felt the sharp blow to his back, until he saw the prong of the pitchfork protruding from his neck several inches below his chin. Instinctively, Billy reached up to try to stop the bleeding, but already his mouth and nose were full of the sticky stuff. He lurched forward on the ladder. Even when he stopped breathing, during a final moment of consciousness, he could smell the sweet, tangy alcohol in his blood, spilling everywhere.

Chapter 14

CALEB WALKED DOWN THE alley behind the diner. He opened the steel door to the kitchen and leaned his head inside. Trinity was sitting on a stool with her back to him, thumbing through the worn and wrinkled pages of a fashion magazine. She was wearing a white T-shirt and cut-off jeans, her hair hanging loosely about her shoulders.

"Pssst."

Trinity turned and flashed him a long, grateful smile, as if she knew that Caleb knew it all and she expected him to save her.

She stood up slowly.

"Trinity…I…"

She put her index finger to her lips.

"Not now," she whispered, "take me for a ride. I want to show you something."

She guided him through town to a narrow, pitted road leading away from the river. As they drove, she closed her eyes and raised her hands in the air above the windshield to catch the wind.

"It's wonderful!" she yelled over the noise. "I don't know how you keep your eyes on the road."

Caleb smiled and shook his head with wonder at her appreciation for something so simple as the open road.

They climbed a hill and turned onto a dirt road. He pulled the car into a thicket where Trinity said no one would see it. Before he could turn the key, she was already out of the car picking her way up a steep, rocky trail.

"C'mon, Caleb," she urged between breaths, "follow me."

Occasionally, Trinity slipped and stumbled on the loose stone. Caleb reached out to steady her, but quickly stopped himself. She was clearly used to making her own way without much help. He did not want to belittle her effort by treating her any differently now.

When he reached the top just behind Trinity, he found himself on a small outcropping of rock that afforded a sweeping view of the land as far as the eye could see. The hills and misty fields rolled softly to the horizon like a gentle green tide. Except for the church steeple in town and the bridge beyond that, there was no sign humans had ventured into this land.

Trinity raised her arms to the clear blue sky again. She laughed and danced as she had in the diner when Caleb first saw her. Then she reached out and grabbed his hand. He stared into her deep, murky, brown eyes.

"Don't tell me you came back because you were afraid for me. Tell me you came back because you couldn't help yourself, because you had to be near me."

Caleb looked down and took a step back.

"Are you one of them?" he asked. "Are you trapped here too?"

Trinity sighed. She wrapped her arms around herself and gazed out into the distance.

"We always owe them more money for the rent and the stuff we buy," she spoke softly while her back was turned. "None of us can go till we pay our debts." She took a deep breath. "Yeah, I guess you could say I was trapped here."

Caleb walked around in front of her, but she stared through him, as if searching for something beyond.

"Leave with me. I'll get you help, I'll bring the police, the press. We could let everybody know what's happening here."

Trinity began to sob.

"As soon as they know I'm gone, they'll have the sheriff hurt my mother and the rest. Sometimes, when I'm alone in my bed at night, I wish my mother would have a heart attack and that I would find her in the morning with a peaceful look on her face, dead and gone. She's not much, none of us are, but she's all I got, and I'm not leaving until I know she's gonna be all right. Everybody else too; some of them are my friends."

Then she smiled, vibrant and excited, once again slipping into a curious child's skin.

"Have you ever been to a big city, like New York?"

Caleb nodded.

"I live in Philadelphia."

She gasped.

"Have you ever been to the ocean?"

"Yes, many times."

"I never have been anywhere, except Alabama and here. I grew up on a farm. My dad and mom worked there. When I was fourteen, they told me we were moving for better jobs. I've been here ever since."

"Where is your dad?"

"He left, or he tried to. He walked away one day, he was gonna get help for us, like you say you're gonna do. We never heard from him again. Mom thinks he found another woman and ran off. But she won't face the truth. I know he's dead. I know they caught him. I see him in my dreams sometimes, he talks to me."

"What does he say?"

"He keeps sayin' the same thing over and over again."

Trinity was sobbing again.

"He says, 'All I did was walk away, I just walked away.'"

Caleb felt dizzy, his heart racing. *Could it be the same man, the one Pete's friend found in the field?* Caleb sat down and leaned back on his elbows to steady himself.

Caleb wondered how he had fallen into this sheer madness, this world that time forgot. He found himself longing for a place at the bar in the dark, sipping a cold beer. He missed the routine of his life in Philadelphia. He missed the people with blank stares who passed him on street. They never asked anything of him, or even noticed him at all.

Sensing his anxiety, Trinity rested a hand on his shoulder to comfort him. It felt warm and soft on his skin.

"You can go away right now and pretend you never even met me. I mean that's okay. I've survived so far, I'll get by a little longer. This isn't your problem. I even got a way planned across the river, an old path nobody knows about."

Caleb shook his head.

"It's my problem now, that's for sure," he mumbled.

They both sat in silence for a moment, staring into the deep sky.

Trinity leaned close.

"You never did say why you came here."

"A friend owns a house here, he asked me to stay while he was gone. Do you know the McCoy house, outside of town?"

She reared her head back in disbelief.

"I never been in that one, but I been told about it. I heard it was haunted by the ghosts of the McCoys. I guess they were all evil. I heard they used to bring black slaves up there and make 'em work till they died, back durin' the Civil War."

Caleb stood up and brushed the grass off his shorts.

"This is what I'll do," Caleb said, thinking aloud. "I'll take you back now. Tomorrow, I'll go by myself, to the newspapers first, then the FBI, I guess. I'll bring people back with me."

"Do you really think anyone will care?"

Caleb shot Trinity a curious glance. He had not considered that possibility before. He could not imagine though why the press at least would not be interested. True, he had no proof of murder or violence, but surely a story about a town that made slaves out of the poor and unfortunate would make for great headlines, maybe even a tacky made-for-TV movie.

"Someone will," he whispered.

Caleb glanced at her prosthetic leg while she stood next to him. He bent down, then reached out and touched his fingers to the hard, hollow plastic.

"And how did this happen?" he asked while he looked up at her, squinting against the hot sun.

She quickly pulled her leg back out of his reach.

"Don't, I don't let no one touch it. It's ugly and it hurts all the time."

She explained that she slipped and fell while climbing a tree when she was just a little girl. The leg was so badly broken that it had to be amputated below the knee.

"It wasn't even done in the hospital. We didn't have enough money. The doctor came from Bally to do it, real cheap I guess. I remember waking up on my bed. There was a pair of crutches there my father made for me. I'll never forget what it was like to look down and see nothin' but air. It took me almost a month to get up and use the crutches."

Trinity bent forward and gently rapped her knuckles on the plastic limb.

"They gave me this not long after I came here, so I can work cleaning their houses. But they charged my mom two years rent for it. It's not even the right size, it's a little big. I think it was used by someone else before me."

Suddenly Caleb was so exhausted he had to practically hold his eyelids open. He yawned.

"Don't take me home," she pleaded. "Just take me back to my mom, she'll be gettin' off work soon. I don't want her worryin' about all this. I don't want her to even know what you're thinkin'."

Trinity let Caleb help her back down to the car, his arm around her waist. Her body was lean and hard from work. She smelled like fresh rain. It took all his will to keep from imagining her naked, moving gently beneath him while they made love. He thought he saw her smiling once, amused by his torture.

Neither one of them spoke much on the way back. Trinity leaned close to him sometimes, then lightly touched the back of his neck for a moment. Caleb meanwhile was thinking about what he would say when he got back to the civilized world, how he would explain what he'd found in Promise. In the absence of any real proof, he would have a hard time convincing anyone that there were indentured servants kept in the home state of Bruce Springsteen. But he at least had to try.

When Caleb dropped her off, Trinity kissed him on the cheek with soft lips.

"I know I'll see you soon," she whispered.

Chapter 15

WHEN CALEB GOT BACK to the house, he let Sara out. She immediately ran off toward the clearing and the strange mound. By the time Caleb caught up with her, she was digging furiously once more.

"Goddamit!" he yelled. 'Knock it off!"

Caleb was in no mood for distractions. But Sara ignored him, driven by scent and thousands of years of instincts to tear apart the ground. Exhausted and frustrated, Caleb reached out and pulled her suddenly by the collar so hard that she yelped and rolled over at his feet submissively. Then he looked into the hole.

Something, long and narrow, was packed tightly in the dirt several inches below the surface. At first, Caleb thought it was an exposed root, but when he bent down for a closer look, he could see streaks of white where Sara had scratched off the grime with her nails.

Caleb reached in and grabbed hold of it. It was dense and hard like steel, certainly not a root. He could feel it move when he yanked on it, loosening. Finally, he pulled on it with both hands until it broke free in a spray of sandy dirt, the force throwing him back on his behind.

It was a bone, about eight inches long with bulbs on either end notched to fit against another length of bone. He decided that the impact of the fallen limb had forced it up close enough to the surface for his dog to sense it. He examined it closely. Maybe it belonged to a bear or deer or some other large animal, perhaps a horse. Still, a thorny suspicion tugged at the back of his mind; something was not right.

Caleb dug with his fingers and found another bone, similar to the first, only smaller. He dropped to his knees and frantically clawed at the soft ground. One after the other, of almost every shape and size, he pulled them from the ground.

Then he found the skull.

He held the sphere in his hands, using his fingers to scratch off clumps of dirt that still clung to it. The old bone shone softly in the light, almost glowing. He looked into the empty, lifeless eye sockets. The bones around the facial area were pushed inward in a concave shape, as if the person had been hit with something heavy and hard.

Caleb glanced around, and then his eyes followed the contour of the rising ground to very top of the strange mound.

"Oh my God," he whispered.

Caleb dropped the skull and ran back to the barn. He found a rusty axe just inside the doorway and he chopped at the dirt. Bones, skulls, even dirt-encrusted belt buckles and the soles of shoes seemed to erupt from the mound, the pressure of years forcing them to the surface like a brown volcano. It was as if even the earth rejected these lost souls, as if it demanded that Caleb discover their fate before they would be allowed to rest peacefully.

Caleb began to pant. Light and shadows swirled together at blinding speed, spinning out of control. He fell, gasping for air. The bones were all around, tickling him, clawing at him. The skulls whispered about their lives while they rolled into the pile, searching for their extremities. Caleb shut his eyes and buried his face in the cool grime.

"A dream," he whispered.

Confused and disoriented, he stumbled back to the house like a drunken sailor. Even through the blinding orange glare of the afternoon sun he could make out the figure of a man standing in the driveway.

"You are Caleb Magellan?"

Caleb stopped, still panting and soaked with sweat.

"Yes."

The man stepped forward. A gold badge sparkled. The nametag read "Millstone."

"You're from Philadelphia, right?"

Caleb nodded.

His face was thin. His nose was long and narrow. His eyes were black, set deeply in his face. He had the look of an eagle or hawk, cunning and vicious, always in search of a kill.

He smiled mockingly.

"Look at you, you look like you've been rolling around with pigs."

Caleb nodded once more, then glanced down at his filthy clothing.

"I was out in the barn...cleaning the stalls."

Millstone donned a cowboy hat, tilting it forward just enough to shade his eyes. He rested his hands on his hips.

"I bet you're wondering why I'm here," he said while he gazed out over the lake.

He was playing with Caleb, waiting for a guilty conscience to reveal itself. Caleb exhaled a deep sigh of relief. If Millstone had known that Caleb was privy to the town's dark dealings, he would not have bothered with the pleasantries. He would already be in prison, or worse.

"I guess I'm the stranger in town and you're checking up on me?"

Millstone shot Caleb an intense, accusing glare.

"That's right. I saw your car in town. I checked your plate. I asked around. Some people said they saw you comin' up here. The question now becomes what the hell are you doin' here?"

"I'm staying here while the owner, Maximillian McCoy, is in Atlanta on business. His son asked me to come."

Millstone took another step forward, his hand moving to the butt of his sidearm. His beady eyes opened wide as if he had been electro-cuted.

"When did you talk to Frazier?" he demanded.

"A week ago I saw him in Philadelphia."

Millstone dropped his head and laughed quietly.

"I bet you haven't talked to him lately though, right?"

Caleb paused.

"No, I don't know where he is now. But I have his phone number if you want it."

Millstone shook his head.

"No, I don't need it. But I'm gonna check into this nonetheless, you stayin' here I mean."

He threw his hat through the window of his car onto the seat, then climbed in. Before he shut the door, he leaned out.

"I'll be back in the morning. I don't want you goin' anywhere in the meantime."

Caleb nodded and smiled to assure him that he understood. All he needed was a few more hours and he would be gone, back across the border into Pennsylvania. But he had no doubt that if he ran into Mill-stone again, the result would be violent. He did not want to give him cause to come back any sooner.

Chapter 16

"Yes?" the deep voice on the other end of the phone responded.

For a moment, Millstone said nothing while he composed his thoughts. The connection crackled with static. Millstone knew that Mr. McCoy did not appreciate stuttering or bumbling; he wanted a concise appraisal of the situation, as he always seemed to have little time or attention to devote to Millstone's concerns.

"Mr. McCoy, it's Sheriff Millstone."

"Sheriff, you know that I am here on business. You better have a good reason for interrupting me, as I was about to address a group of potential investors."

Millstone launched into the story about finding Caleb Magellan on the property, and how Magellan told him he had permission to be on the grounds from Frazier.

"You assured me, Sheriff, that my son would no longer be capable of causing us difficulty."

"This was before the, well…accident. Anyway, I sent deputies to the house to keep an eye on him. I disconnected the phone in case he tried to call anyone else."

Millstone was pleased with himself, having taken action so swiftly to contain the outsider.

"Is there any truth to what this guy says, should I take him into custody?"

"No, don't arrest him, he would certainly be a liability sitting in our jail. I want you to find out if he knows anything, then I want you to bury him and everyone or everything he came with."

The line was silent for a moment.

"Once you have spoken with this Mr. Magellan, I want you to call me with an update."

"I understand sir."

"Make sure you inform the Council as well, Sheriff. I want them to spread the word that we may have a problem. Tell them that everyone should be watching for anything unusual, and that they should report anything odd to you."

"I'll get on it, Mr. McCoy."

"Make sure you do."

"Anything else, sir?"

"Yes. I'll be leaving on a plane tonight, seven thirty. Make sure you have somebody waiting for me."

"Yes sir."

Millstone hung up the cellular phone, pushed the antenna down and put it back in his shirt pocket. He rolled down the window to his cruiser and inhaled deeply in the cool shadow left behind by the setting sun.

He felt alive, important, powerful and lustful. He was in charge and he would decide who would live tonight and who would die, and this excited him beyond his limited ability to articulate his state of mind. But none of that mattered anyway because words were for pussy faggots like the late Frazier McCoy. He was a man of action. Where morality and fear prevented other people from doing what they wanted, he had none. He acted on his instincts, and he was the greatest man in the world. He smiled to himself in the rear view mirror to be sure it was not all just a wonderful dream.

He started the car and pulled out onto the road. But he would make his way slowly to the McCoy house, relishing every inch of the road, every second that ticked away, every tickle of anticipation of the force he was going to dish out. He rested his hand on his pistol while he drove because it was more fun to touch and stroke than his own dick.

Chapter 17

CALEB STOOD IN THE dark foyer, his heavy breaths echoing loudly. In the faces on the wall, in this house, he knew he would find the answers. He remembered the locked door on the second floor.

He climbed the stairs and stood outside the door for a moment, watching the sweat and dirt drip off his head and fall onto the ornate oriental carpet.

He tried the knob, then leaned against the door, testing its strength. Caleb stood back, ready to throw himself against the door. Then he stopped and began to pace back and forth just in front of it.

"What the fuck am I doing?" He screamed and shook his fists.

Caleb knew that if he broke into the room, there would be no turning back. He did not practice criminal law, but he guessed that would be a crime, or at least an act that would require a formal explanation. But he had no idea what he was really looking for until he saw it. And he needed something, some proof other than old bones to support a tale that would otherwise sound like nothing but the ravings of a lunatic.

Then he turned away from the door to leave it all behind.

After all, he could be home in a couple of hours, just in time to get to Shiny's and get his usual seat at the bar. Two more hours, he thought, and I'll be sipping ice cold Guinness and this place will be nothing but a bad fucking dream. So what if he went back to the crappy city and his shoebox apartment? At least he knew his way around there, even if that life made him miserable.

He started down the ornate stairwell with his things, but stopped once again. He buried his face in his grimy hands. On the back of his eyelids he saw Trinity staring back at him desperately. Something swelled and quivered in his stomach. Could it be attraction, pity, admiration, respect, maybe even love? It was a little bit of everything he decided, and he would not leave her behind. And it was about time his life was about something other than himself and his petty musings. There were a lot of people here, both alive and dead, who had to be known and judged by the world. He knew the truth, or at least part of it, and that would have to do.

Maybe, he thought, he had no control over what he was about to do. He could not help but feel like his actions were being directed from a distant place. Perhaps he was only a weapon wielded by the tortured souls who once owned the shattered and decomposing bones he found in the field. As much as Caleb justified his decision upon love or duty, a naked, scalding desire for revenge consumed him.

Caleb found himself in front of the locked door once more. He drew back, and then charged it like a madman, using all his weight behind his shoulder. The door flexed and cracked, but did not give way. Once more, he drew back, focusing all his anger, fear and frustration on the simple piece of wood that kept him from what he was not supposed to know. He screamed and hurled himself against the door. This time, it came completely off its hinges and Caleb fell into the study and tumbled across the floor.

The room smelled like cologne and cigar smoke. The walls were covered with burgundy leather tacked into place with brass nails. It matched two high-backed chairs facing a large mahogany desk with an identical chair behind it. Diplomas displayed on the wall announced that Frazier's father, Maximillian McCoy, had graduated from the University of Mississippi and Harvard Law School.

Caleb rifled through the desk drawers. He found scraps of paper with phone numbers and initials scrawled on them. He found a small combination calendar and address book that he stuffed in his back pocket for no other reason than it appeared private and important.

Caleb pulled on the last drawer on the bottom but it was locked. He grabbed a small marble bust of Stonewall Jackson that sat on the desk and smashed it against the top of the drawer until the wood splintered. He pulled on the knob with both hands once more and the drawer slid open.

He found a ledger with numbers in columns that meant absolutely nothing to him, but he tore out the pages, folded them and stuffed them into his pocket. In the back of the drawer, he found a photo album and another leather-bound ledger with a cracked and flaking cover, probably much older than the first. He sat down in the plush desk chair while he paged through the album.

On each page, under plastic, was a different faded, yellow newspaper article reporting the mandate of the Confederate Congress during the Civil War that all slaves who were found in the service of the Union army must be executed, rather than taken prisoner. None of it made any sense. He opened the old ledger.

Inside the cover was the name, "M. McCoy." On the first page, at the top of the first column was the word "Date." The top of the second column read "Number Slaves." The top of the third column read "Amount Gold." The first date inscribed in the ledger was January 2nd, 1862. In the second column, the corresponding entry was "17." Next to it, in the third column was the number "14." On and on, until the last entry on December 9th, 1864, the ledger described what appeared to be the sale of human beings for gold. Slavery. And Marcus McCoy, the noble founder of Promise, was involved. Although he had left the South, apparently he had not left his lifestyle behind. Instead, he no doubt carried his business to the North on the backs of slaves, under the very noses of the abolitionists. Caleb was virtually certain that the bones he found had to be the remains of the slave laborers who lived and died here.

Caleb quickly gathered up the album and the ledger and put them in his duffle bag. While he packed the rest of his things, he anticipated the roar of his Stingray as it chewed up the highway and carried him and Trinity anywhere that he could find streetlights and people. He hoisted the duffle bag over his shoulder and bounded down the twisting stairwell with Sara in tow. He passed the dark portraits. Angry ancient eyes followed him, cursed him. Caleb met them face-to-face.

"Fuck you," he muttered under his breath as he walked.

Caleb reached for the doorknob. Something made him look over his shoulder before he left. The urns. He examined them once more for a moment. Then it hit him like a speeding freight train. He suddenly remembered. *The cemetery, the voices, the obelisk. The name on the grave was McCoy! Why would they have grave markers if they were cremated and their ashes sitting right here? They wouldn't likely be buried and cremated!*

Caleb let his duffel bag fall to the floor. Slowly he approached the portrait of Marcus McCoy. He had to know what was in the jars. He grabbed the clay urn and pulled the knob of the lid. Nothing. He scraped away the wax that sealed it, but still it would not budge.

Caleb raised the heavy urn above his head then released his grip. In a cloud of gray dust it shattered on the marble floor. There, among the shards of pottery, he found the horrifying evidence of a crime far more terrible than the mere subjugation of human beings. He found the trophies of mass murder.

His hands trembling, he raised up a piece of leather string from the dust. Attached to the string were what he first thought were old prunes or apricots, but on closer examination he could not mistake the teardrop shape of severed human ears. Hundreds, maybe even thousands of them he found as he uncoiled string after string that had been packed tightly, deliberately in the jar.

Caleb stood up, swaying. He was feverish, lightheaded, yet at the same time feeling as though hot, heavy molten lead flowed through his veins. He swiped another urn off its pedestal. Among the shattered pieces he found more of the same dried, leathery evidence of what he feared so desperately. One by one he smashed them all to find they were choked full of the moldy, mummified ears.

While Caleb fought back the surge of vomit burning the back of his throat, he made another sickening observation. They were all right ears. It all came together.

Marcus McCoy had systematically executed the wretched slaves who came here, and he did it for the money. The ledger was proof of it. He must have cut off the ears of each victim, sending the left one of the pair on and keeping the other, a grisly but accurate receipt.

The Confederate government had paid him handsomely to insure that any slaves who made their way north would not be enlisted to fight against it. For a moment, Caleb allowed himself to be one of them in his mind, traveling treacherous miles to a place of freedom only to reach this sticky death factory. Everyone who lived in Promise at that time became rich while they conducted a secret massacre. After the blood flowed, they surely greeted each and smiled, knowing they were together but alone, bound in their secret for eternity. And no doubt, everyone who lived here now could thank their murderous ancestors for their trust funds and dark, towering houses.

Caleb emptied the clothes out of his bag and carefully, respectfully, replaced them with as many of the fragile severed ears as he could fit without crushing them, the last vestiges of so many tragic lives. Yet, this evidence was indisputable. And they would kill him over it.

Caleb opened the front door and managed a grateful smile as he glimpsed his car glowing in the twilight, the vehicle of his freedom. But when he stepped outside, he saw a sheriff's car blocking the driveway. The porcine figure of one of Millstone's deputies was staring out across the lake. Fortunately, he was apparently drawn in and distracted by its sparkling beauty.

Caleb gasped, whirled around and dove back inside the house. Quietly, slowly, as if even the slightest vibration or noise might set off an explosion, he pushed the door shut and locked it. He slung his bag over his shoulder. Caleb rifled through the pockets of his jeans until he found Pete's phone number. He fought off the panic and dizziness long enough to crawl into the kitchen. He snatched the phone off the kitchen counter. He could not risk calling the police or an ambulance or any other entity of government; chances were that everybody in a position of authority within a hundred miles was in the pocket of Maximillian McCoy. But he could count on Pete, he was sure of that.

He dialed, but when he put the phone to his ear there was nothing, not even static. The lines had been cut. They had cut him off from contact with the outside world that he had longed to disown only a few days before.

Caleb curled up in a ball on the floor and began to sob.

Chapter 18

CALEB WAS SPINNING OUT of control. He tried to remain calm, but he could not quell the panic.

He shivered and panted, on the verge of passing out. His muscles were coiled, cramped and frozen. Sara stood over him and whined, sensing his fear. He was certain that Millstone and his deputies would burst through the door any second and put a sudden violent end to his shame. His father was right. He was a coward.

Caleb fought his body, his mind, his father. He clenched his fists and pounded them on the floor. Ironically, the searing pain in his hands seemed to snuff out the raging fire in his mind. It was as if he were watching himself on a computer screen, directing his own movements from some remote location. His fear still made his heart pound, but he could act in spite of it.

Caleb searched each kitchen drawer, throwing the contents on the floor. His hands found the cold steel in the back of the last drawer, and he slowly removed the pistol, astonished by its weight in his hands. His finger found the trigger and he examined it in the light. It was a large caliber stainless steel revolver. He had no idea how to handle a gun, but he knew how to point it and squeeze the trigger.

Caleb ran back to the front door and peeked through the curtains. There were three, including Millstone. He was gesturing to the other two, directing them around the house. They nodded and disappeared from view.

They were trying to surround him.

Caleb ran back through the kitchen and whistled for Sara to follow him. He jogged down the hallway from the kitchen to the rear door. If he could get out before they took up their positions, they would never even know he was gone. He opened the door and was as surprised to see the fat deputy as he was to see Caleb.

They both froze. Caleb searched his wide eyes for clues about what he might do, but they told him little except that he was a mindless follower who would rather see Caleb dead than live in world where he would be nothing more than a gas station attendant.

Shaking, the fat man reached for the gun at his side. Caleb raised his arm revealing his own weapon while the deputy still fumbled with his gun, trying to pull it out of the holster. He froze again, no doubt wondering if Caleb would really shoot him before he could draw.

"Don't do it," Caleb whispered. "Let me go."

The deputy was trembling, but he freed his gun and began to raise it up to Caleb's chest.

Caleb pulled the trigger and the entire world exploded in a blinding flash and deafening boom that sent him reeling to the floor, dazed. When he finally managed to pull himself back up, a cloud of gray smoke and the hot peppery smell of gunpowder greeted him.

The deputy was on his knees just outside the door. His gun was still in his hand. He was trying to crawl away, while at the same time grabbing at his chest where the bullet had struck. Blood was streaming from the wound down his shirt and formed a crimson trail behind him. He turned around and looked at Caleb and gurgled some sound as bright red foam bubbled and dripped from the corners of his mouth.

But then he looked back through Caleb, focusing on something behind him in the distance, or perhaps in another world. Maybe it was the black robe of death he saw, sweeping across the sun, coming for him. Whatever he beheld, it frightened him and he crawled faster. He looked back once more, his face twisted with terror, and then he dropped in an amorphous pile of flesh, motionless and dead.

Caleb did not have much opportunity to ponder all the moral and legal repercussions of killing a man, especially a lawman. He was now an animal, gnashing his teeth and fighting for his own life. He would gladly see them all lying in a pool of blood before he would breathe his last. He jumped over the body and sprinted across the lawn.

Caleb instinctively whirled around just in time to see Millstone taking aim at him from around a corner.

"No!" Caleb grunted through clenched teeth.

Millstone only smiled politely.

Caleb closed his eyes, raised his gun up once again and blindly pulled the trigger. Millstone's gun fired simultaneously, but with much greater accuracy.

Caleb felt the bone-crushing blow to his leg, and his whole body went numb. He was falling, spinning through the air. He imagined that he had jumped from a plane, only to realize that he had forgotten his parachute. Dizzy, still spinning, he hit the ground.

Millstone stood over Caleb, prodding and poking at him with the toe of one of his boots,

"You ain't dead, but you're gonna' wish you were before I get done."

Caleb opened his eyes. His head and his leg throbbed so that each felt as if it had its own pounding heart. Caleb tried to talk, but the words eluded him like butterflies that he grasped for with his bare hands.

"Awwww, isn't that sweet," Millstone remarked sarcastically while he gestured with his gun. "Your doggie still loves you."

Caleb propped himself up on his elbows. Sara was crouched down just a few feet away, coiled and growling, waiting to strike. As carelessly and effortlessly as one would toss a pebble or wave away a gnat, Millstone swung his gun up and fired. Sara spun around and yelped, then tumbled to the ground. She pulled herself along the ground with her front paws to edge of the yard, then disappeared into the brush and shadows. Millstone fired another shot. Caleb heard a few high-pitched whimpers that faded more each time. Then there was nothing, except the wind and the sky and Sara's invisible ghost rocketing to heaven.

Caleb's grief and rage spurred him to action. While Millstone stood over him and thought of something else clever to say, Caleb reached up and grabbed his testicles. He wrenched, twisted and pulled at them with all the strength he could muster. Instinctively, Millstone groaned and reached down with both hands to ward off the attack. When he did, Caleb snatched the gun from his hand and fired a shot where he thought Millstone's head should be. But he had already ducked, rolling to the side and crawling for cover around the corner of the house. Caleb fired wildly at him while he moved, but all of the bullets missed, striking the house and splintering the wood siding.

Caleb climbed to his feet and briefly examined his wound. The bullet had skimmed his calf, taking with it a large chunk of skin and muscle. He took a step and the pain shot through his body like lightning. He screamed and took another shaky step, then another. With tears in his eyes, he stumbled across the yard and the driveway to the winding trail that led through the forest. He could hear Millstone shouting at the other deputy. A shot whizzed by, crashing into the trees above him.

Caleb fell several times in the thick underbrush while he searched for the skinny brown ribbon of dirt. Another shot rang out, but it came nowhere near him. Although he could hear them stomping through the brush, they had apparently lost sight of him among the leaves. When he found the path, he limped off at a slow jog, gaining precious moments on Millstone and his deputy.

He had lost Millstone's gun sometime during the chase, but it mattered little because the sounds of his pursuers faded in the distance behind him. Finally, when he could see the mirrored surface of the clear pool, he stopped. For a moment, he listened. All he could hear now was the breath of the forest moving lazily through the trees.

Caleb sat down and slid his wounded leg into the frigid water. Slowly, gently, he probed the bullet hole with his fingers, to clean away the dried blood and bits of dirt that had worked their way into it. He clenched his teeth to keep from uttering any sound that might give his position away, but he could not hold back the tears that streamed down his face. He suddenly became so unsteady and tired that he had to lean back on the ground. The orange light that shone through gaps in the treetops became fuzzy and pale, obscured by a fog of pain. By the time he realized that he was fainting, he was too exhausted to care. All he needed was a couple of minutes of shuteye, he thought, and then he would be back on his way.

It seemed that only a split second later somebody was trying to wake him.

"Wake up asshole," Millstone bellowed while he jammed the heel of his cowboy boot into the side of Caleb's head. "You've got some talkin' to do before you die."

Instinctively, Caleb covered his head with his hands and arms.

"Good, you ain't dead."

Caleb rolled over and began to crawl away, but Millstone kicked him in the side. Caleb could hear a muffled crack. He collapsed and howled in agony.

"C'mon Cy," Millstone motioned to the other deputy. "Let's get him up."

Millstone slung a shotgun over his shoulder, then he and the other deputy each grabbed one of Caleb's arms and hauled him up off the ground.

"Why don't we just kill him, Sheriff? He already killed Freddy."

"Because we've got to find out what he knows, you idiot, and what he told anybody else. Besides, he's gonna be my gift to Mr. McCoy when he gets in. I want him alive for that."

"But what about Freddy, he killed Freddy!"

Millstone grabbed his stunned deputy by his shirt and pulled him close.

"I just told you the reason, you dumb fuck. Besides, that tub of shit was never good for anything anyway. He was fat and stupid, that's what got him dead."

Millstone released his grip then motioned toward Caleb with a sweeping hand.

"Grab a leg, let's get him back to the house."

Caleb struggled to free himself while they dragged him out of the forest, but each time he squirmed, Millstone jabbed him in the ribs and he collapsed with pain.

Millstone and his deputy carried him around to the back of the house. The deputy held a gun to Caleb's head while Millstone swung open a set of metal doors leading to a basement. Millstone walked back over, grabbed Caleb by his hair and dragged him down a flight of stairs into the darkness.

"Stay a while," Millstone whispered. "I'll be back."

With a resounding clang, the doors swung closed, shutting out even the tiniest pinhole of light. Caleb could smell the dampness as he felt along the moist, flaking walls. He tripped over something and fell onto the dirt floor. When he had warded off the wave of shuddering pain, he remembered he had a pack of matches in his pocket. Several of them were soaked with sweat and refused to ignite, but luckily, one of them erupted into a warm glowing flame.

The room was small, probably an old root cellar. It was empty except for some concrete blocks and some old burlap sacks. Caleb noticed something carved on one of the walls. He had to light another match and hold it close to make out what it said. "Franklin Carver."

The letters varied in size and shape, as if written by a child. Caleb felt the grooves with his fingers. They were scratched deep into the plaster.

He piled up the remains of the burlap sacks on the ground and reclined to await his fate. In the quiet dark, his mind raced and churned, struggling to erect a barrier against reality.

The scenes changed rapidly, unpredictably, as if pieces of his memory had been spliced together randomly to form a grainy, sputtering film.

He was a child, crying. He was reaching out for his mother, grasping for her. A curtain was blowing in an open window. His father stood with his back to Caleb, reading a newspaper. He turned around. But it was Caleb's own face, his own voice that screamed for him to be quiet.

Then he was swimming, far from shore. He pumped his arms harder, but he drifted further away. Exhausted, he sank to the muddy bottom. But he found he could breathe in the water as easily as he breathed the air above. Elated, he swam with the fish and marveled at sunken ships. He picked through their scattered contents, searching for gold and silver.

Seamlessly, the scene changed yet again. He was standing in a field. Sara stalked something in the distance. Caleb yelled for her at the top of his lungs, but she disappeared. He ran after her, but he kept falling. He cried and pounded the ground.

Caleb's body twitched and a wave of pain crashed over him. He was awake, tears streaming down his face.

He felt a sharp, pricking pain in the middle of his back. He reached back and found a rusty nail about three or four inches long partially buried in the dirt.

He rolled over onto his stomach, then lit another match. He began to carve his own name on the wall next to Franklin Carver's. Maybe, he thought, when he was long dead, rotting away in an unmarked grave, someone might find his mark and wonder what had happened to him.

When he was finished, he leaned back and drifted in and out of blackness, somewhere between sleep and death. There were no images this time, only a stillness that seemed to last forever while at the same time evaporating in the blink of an eye.

The doors swung open.

It was night, and its familiar sounds found their way into the room. Caleb squinted against the soft moonlight. The moon's primordial lure was suddenly clear and compelling. He wanted to sit on it and judge the puny world like a god.

Millstone appeared in the doorway. He turned his head, revealing his sharp features in profile. He nodded to some unseen presence out of Caleb's sight. He turned on a flashlight and directed the beam into Caleb's eyes.

"Get up, boy."

Pushing against the wall for support, Caleb climbed to his feet. Millstone pointed a shotgun at him waist-high.

Another figure descended the stairs into the cellar. He was tall enough that he had to duck his head to avoid striking the top of the doorway. He seemed to tower over Millstone, who was at least six feet tall.

"I'm Maximillian McCoy." He spoke in a deep, educated voice as if he were a politician introducing himself to a crowd on a street corner. "You are, no doubt, Caleb Magellan," he continued, stepping forward out of the glare of light where Caleb could see his face.

His head was large and his face was long and drawn downward, giving him a constant expression of dissatisfaction. Like his portrait, his eyes were cold yet intelligent, suggesting the same cunning that brought Marcus McCoy great power over men and their affairs. His face was clean-shaven and his gray hair was receding, exacerbating his hard, haughty air.

"Hmmph," he breathed while he squinted, examining Caleb from head to toe.

He turned to Millstone.

"It's hard to believe this wreck of man could prove to be so much trouble for us," he turned back to Caleb, "or for my poor son Frazier. He's dead now, did you know that?"

Caleb cocked his head curiously.

Maximillian McCoy tapped his chest with his index finger while he spoke.

"Oh yes, Mr. Magellan, I had him killed because he threatened to expose me, his own father!"

Then he thrust his hands in his pants pockets.

"Do you think I would deal with you any less harshly?"

Caleb wiped his nose with the back of his hand.

"What the hell are you talking about?"

Caleb thought that by playing stupid he could buy some time. He had no plan, but he prayed something might come to him.

Maximillian McCoy locked his hands behind his back and paced slowly back and forth while he spoke.

"You see, you were not supposed to be here, and Frazier knew this. We are a very tightly knit family, and we have interests to protect, interests that are, shall we say, unique to our heritage. An outsider like you certainly would not understand our situation. An outsider like you might be inclined to involve other outside parties in our affairs. People who would be inclined to condemn us." He stared at the ceiling for a moment, composing his thoughts. "I think you know what things I am talking about, don't you?"

Caleb did not possess the strength or reason to formulate any answer.

Maximillian McCoy continued pacing.

"But he was your son," Caleb finally managed to whisper.

"Biologically, that is correct, but he was not one of us. He was a liability. The fact that you and I are now in the same room proves it. In any event, let's talk about you. Tell me what you think my dealings are?"

Caleb shook his head.

"I don't know."

"That is not true. I found my things in your luggage, and the Sheriff showed me what you dug up in the pasture. The question is, are you smart enough to put two and two together?"

Caleb shook his head once more.

"I don't know what you are talking about."

"Let me put it to you this way. Mr. Magellan, you are already dead. It's simply a matter now of the good Sheriff putting a bullet in your brain, or breaking every bone in your body and then putting a bullet in your brain."

He stopped a few feet in front of Caleb and folded his arms.

"You see, if you tell me everything and convince me that you have not contacted anybody else about what you know, I may let the others live, even that crippled girl."

Caleb gasped.

"Why, Mr. Magellan, you seem surprised. You see, I know everything that goes on in this town, or should I say the Sheriff does, and he relays that information to me."

He grabbed Caleb by the throat with one of his big hands. His hot breath smelled like musk aftershave and alcohol. Fire danced in his blue, fathomless eyes.

"Don't think for one second I won't burn them all alive while they sleep and then piss on the ashes, Mr. Magellan," he growled through clenched teeth. "If you know anything about me by now, you know that I will not hesitate to protect what is mine, what my ancestors built."

He released his grip and stood back again.

"Well, what is it going to be? Just you, or shall they all die? Tell me now what you know."

Caleb sighed, defeated.

"I know that you keep slaves here in this town somehow," Caleb spoke while he slid down the wall, sitting down on the dirt floor. "I know that your ancestors murdered slaves here during the Civil War, and buried them in the field out there. I think they were paid by the Confederates for it, to keep the slaves out of the war."

Maximillian McCoy smiled.

"That's pretty close to the truth. I am impressed by your intelligence, Mr. Magellan, at having put all that together from an old ledger, some bones and dried up flesh."

He began to pace back and forth again while he narrated the tale.

"It was not murder as you put it, Mr. Magellan. It was war. Marcus McCoy was loyal to the South. He viewed himself as a patriot of the cause, but because he was too old to fight he did what he could to help. When the slaves came north by the Underground Railroad, he established himself as one of their benefactors. At first, he saw to it that they were sent back to their owners. But when the Confederates deemed them to be a threat to the extent they could take up arms against them, my great-great-grandfather answered the call. He killed them by the thousands, and he was paid in Confederate gold for his efforts. As you probably guessed, he cut off their ears. He kept the right ear, but sent on the left ear as proof of the deed. Pretty ingenious, don't you think?

"But what you do not know was that when he could no longer handle the flow, the entire town, comprised mostly of his loyal followers, pitched in to finish the job. And so, everyone became rich with gold. Over the years, their offspring, of which I am one, inherited their money and multiplied it. We created an empire of land, stock and trusts founded on Marcus McCoy's loyalty."

"They were innocent and you murdered them."

"No." Maximillian McCoy shouted and shook a clenched fist. "They were combatants who would have killed good boys of the South!"

"What about now?" Caleb shouted back. "You keep slaves now and you kill them when they try to leave!"

"They are weak, human garbage who would otherwise be out robbing liquor stores and molesting children. We have given them a better home than they have ever known. They would have died or gone to prison if not for us anyway."

Caleb buried his face in his hands.

"None of that really matters anyway, Mr. Magellan, because that knowledge will die with you. But there is a silver lining in your black cloud. I do not believe that you spoke to anyone else about what you found. Otherwise, I think my workers would have already tried to escape. In light of that, I will only dispose of the people with whom you had contact, rather than the entire camp." He shrugged his broad shoulders. "Of course that means the crippled girl will not live to see another day."

He motioned for Millstone.

"Take him out to the field and finish him."

As Millstone reached down for him, Caleb exploded. He focused on the tiny bits of strength his body had instinctively stored away for a moment like this. He rose up like a phoenix. He caught Millstone completely by surprise when he grabbed the barrel of the shotgun and pulled hard on it, bringing Millstone to the ground. He planned to bull-rush Maximillian McCoy, get out and lock them both inside. But when he got to his feet, the big man was already on him. Caleb had terribly misjudged his physical prowess. McCoy shoved him into the wall so hard he lost his breath. Caleb grabbed his chest and fell to the ground, gasping for air.

When Millstone recovered, he pointed the gun at Caleb's head and began to squeeze the trigger.

Maximillian McCoy grabbed his arm.

"Not in here, Sheriff," he commanded. This is my home. Take him out to the field and do it, then bury him with all the others."

Millstone hit Caleb hard with the butt of the gun in his broken rib. Caleb began to lose consciousness as the pain flooded his brain and seemed to pour out of his ears. Everything was white and flashing.

He thought he drifted outside of himself while Millstone dragged his limp and battered body across the ground beneath the stars. He could see Millstone occasionally stop to get a better grip on his legs, then continue to pull him along over whatever sticks or sharp rocks he could find. Caleb thought it must have hurt him, but he was relieved that he was not feeling any more of the grueling pain.

When they had reached the crest of the mound in the field where the others had met their fate, Millstone again put the shotgun to Caleb's head. Caleb closed his eyes.

Instead of an explosion, he heard a loud thump. Millstone fell on top of him, his body convulsing.

"You gotta help me," Trinity whispered. "I can't roll him off you by myself."

Caleb pushed and Millstone rolled over onto his back on the ground.

"Trinity, what did you do?"

"Just hit him with a big rock. I heard shots before all the way in the camp. Everyone else was too scared to come."

Trinity lifted his head up.

"Are you hurt bad?"

"He shot me in the leg...I think he cracked my rib too."

"C'mon," she said, trying to pull Caleb to his feet, "we gotta get outta' here."

"No, not me at least. I have to go back to the house, I have to get the proof. But you have to go. McCoy said he was going to kill you for talking to me."

Trinity started to sob.

"Proof of what?" she asked.

"There's a lot more going on here than you could possibly imagine. I'm so sorry Trinity for getting you into this, but I'm going to try to make it right. Go get your mom and everybody else and start walking. You said you knew a way."

She wiped her nose and nodded.

"What about you?"

"I have to go back, I have no choice."

"Why?"

"I'll explain it to you later, when we're sitting on a park bench, reading about it in a newspaper."

He pointed to Millstone's body.

"Hand me his gun. I have to fire a shot so they think Millstone got me. Cover your ears."

Caleb pointed the shotgun into the air, turned his head away and pulled the trigger. The boom resounded across the sky. Caleb examined the gun for a moment, then awkwardly pumped another shell into the firing chamber. He slung the gun over his shoulder. He began to limp back toward the house. Trinity stood still and stared at him.

"Go on," he said. "I'll see you when it's done. I'll find you somehow."

Trinity waved, then disappeared into the shadows.

Chapter 19

CALEB COULD SEE A light in the study as he approached, and he moved quietly through the open door and up the stairs. He had no idea how many shells the gun held, so he simply assumed that he had only one shot, and that it would have to count. But it was a shotgun, so he also understood that his aim did not have to be perfect.

He hugged the wall in the second floor hallway just outside the study. He could hear McCoy on the phone.

"No, I think the problem has been solved, but I do not want to let anyone else know that until I am sure we have disposed of our unwanted guest. I am waiting for Sheriff Millstone to return with what I am confident will be good news. So, for the time being, until you hear from me you must keep everybody on alert."

He hung up the phone, and Caleb stepped inside.

Maximillian McCoy was sitting at the desk shuffling through some of the pieces of paper Caleb had taken out of the desk when he was searching through the drawers.

"I don't want to kill you," Caleb said while he pointed the shotgun at his head, "but I'm not going to let you hurt anyone else."

McCoy looked up. He gawked at Caleb for a second, obviously surprised that he was still alive, but a look of calm confidence quickly returned.

"No matter what happens to me, you're still not going to be able to get away from here." He spoke quietly while he returned to sorting the pieces of paper as if this were just another ordinary day in the course of administering his blood money. "People are watching for you, they will not let you leave. They all have too much to lose if you do."

"Maybe if I take you with me they'll let me go."

"That will not matter, they will kill both of us if they have to. In any event, I will not let that happen. I will not be your hostage; you will have to kill me."

"So be it."

Caleb began to squeeze the trigger, waiting for another shattering explosion that would leave yet another man bleeding, dying and gasping for a last breath. He hesitated a moment too long.

McCoy drew a small pistol from the desk, stood and fired it from his hip. The bullet hit Caleb in the shoulder, the impact sending him to the floor. As Caleb dropped down, he pulled the trigger and the shotgun discharged with a crash like thunder. Before Caleb hit the floor, he saw McCoy fall behind his desk.

Somehow, Caleb crawled into the hallway, resting his back against the other side of the wall. He craned his neck to look at the wound. This time the bullet had barely grazed the skin, leaving only a bloody scratch behind.

He glanced around the corner because he could hear nothing except the ringing in his ears. The shotgun was on the floor. He did not see any movement, and he wondered if he had hit McCoy, maybe even killed him. Caleb squatted down and reached out for the shotgun. That's when he saw Maximillian McCoy lunge at him out of the corner of his eye.

Before Caleb could even react, the big man had landed on his back with all his weight, and began to wrap his strong hands around Caleb's neck.

McCoy screamed while he squeezed, blood streaming down his arm where he had been hit by the shotgun blast. Caleb tried to pry his hands away, but he was no match for the heavier, stronger man. He tried to claw at his wild, raging eyes, but McCoy kept his head just out of Caleb's shorter reach. Caleb began to feel his brain short-circuit from the lack of oxygen. Tiny flash bulbs began to go off all around him. He knew that if he could not get McCoy to relax his grip, he would be dead in a matter of a few terrifying seconds.

In a last desperate, flailing attempt, Caleb searched McCoy's arm for the bullet hole. When he found it, he dug his fingers into the shredded, bloody flesh. McCoy howled and reeled back. Caleb found the shotgun and pulled it in. When he finally got control of it, McCoy was back on top of him again, forcing the gun across his throat and pressing down.

Caleb looked up at him and saw his father. His eyes were bulging and red. He was laughing while drool cascaded down his neck from the corners of his mouth.

Weak little boy, he thought he said. *You never grew up, you never became a man. Spoiled rotten is all you are, soft and rotten.*

Then he took on the freckled, moon-shaped face of Mucus. His unkempt, red hair was falling into his eyes.

I guess you want another beating, chicken. I guess you're getting a little big for your britches. Now I'm gonna knock you down another notch. Why don't you at least fight back this time, at least make it fun for me?

All the emotions Caleb had denied, suppressed or cleverly discounted and ignored, escaped from the prison where he had packed them in. Blinding rage filled his fingers and toes with the energy Caleb had spent to lie to himself over the years. He pushed back against his father and his sidekick, Mucus. He pushed until they stopped laughing, and when he was free he beat them with his fists and his feet and anything else he could find until he was the only one laughing now, and they were the ones dying, begging for mercy.

Caleb found himself standing over the body of Maximillian McCoy. He held the shotgun, blood dripping from it. McCoy's head was oddly misshapen, more flat now than round. He gagged several times, then his body jerked and quivered while a pool of blood spread out on the floor and disappeared into the carpet.

Caleb gathered the papers and the ledger, then made his way downstairs, found his bag and threw it all into the Stingray. He sat in the car and turned the key, but it only sputtered and gasped. He checked under the hood and found cut wires; Millstone's handywork. He looked in the sheriff's car, but the keys were not in the ignition. He would have to walk, but his body ached and burned so badly that every time he took a step, or even breathed, he had to pause for a moment before he could continue.

He sat down in the driveway and leaned against the Stingray. He glanced up at the blanket of night riddled with stars, but it was not the same sky that had fascinated him only several days before. Now, it was cold, dark and distant, a reminder that there was so much to be afraid of.

No matter how much he pinched himself and slapped his cheeks to try to stay awake, he nodded off as his body attempted to recoup some of the energy it had expended.

Chapter 20

AT FIRST, HE THOUGHT he was dreaming, but he heard the sound again and slapped his face hard to be sure he was awake. It was distant, but it sounded as if someone was dragging something across the loose stones in the driveway. Gradually, it drew closer. Caleb stood up, but he could not see anything against the dark landscape. Soon the sound was so near that it seemed to be coming from every direction and no direction at the same time. Something hit him in the back of the legs. He fell and instinctively covered his face. Sara was wagging her tail.

Caleb held her tightly, then examined her carefully. Her right, rear leg was drawn up and tucked underneath her body. Caleb pulled it down a fraction and she whimpered. Millstone's bullet had gone through it and torn a gaping hole near the joint.

Caleb buried his face in her fur while he stroked her neck. She pulled away and licked his face furiously despite the pain she must have been feeling. He closed his eyes. For a minute, nothing had ever happened to them. For a peaceful moment, Sara was chasing birds and groundhogs in the sun-drenched pasture in his mind.

But his playful delusion was quickly interrupted. Headlights sparkled as a car turned slowly off the road and made its way toward the house. Caleb picked up Sara and hid behind the rose bushes in front of the house.

An old pick-up truck with faded letters painted on the door stopped at the end of the cul-de-sac. A man got out. He moved stiffly, gingerly around the truck, swiveling his head in every direction looking for something. He was obviously afraid of what he might find.

Caleb crawled out of the bushes close enough to the truck to read the words, "The General Store" painted on the door.

"Pete!" he moaned in a gravelly voice. "Pete, over here!"

Pete grabbed Caleb by the arms and helped him to his feet.

"My god," he exclaimed, "what the hell happened?"

"Millstone and McCoy are dead. It's a long story, Pete, there isn't time to explain it all now. But you've got to know, everyone in this town is looking for me."

"I saw some people goin' across the old bridge. When I yelled out, they ran like I was going to kill them or somethin'. I had a feeling things went wrong, that's why I came up. But I had to remember what you told me about getting here. I'm lucky I found the place. I called Mr. Kim for company, and he came along. But he told me to drop him in town, the crazy bastard. We'll have to pick him up on the way out if we can find him."

"Was there a girl with them? She would be limping."

"I didn't see no one like that."

Caleb lowered his head.

"I had to do it Pete, they were trying to kill me. You would not believe what's been going on here. I have proof. But...if you try to get me out of here...you might get hurt, you and Kim. I can't ask you to do that."

"C'mon," he said, ignoring the warning.

Caleb was too tired, too delirious to argue. He grabbed his bag from the Stingray then gingerly climbed into Pete's truck that reeked of stale sweat and gasoline.

"Shut off your lights until we get onto the road."

"How bad are you hurt?" he asked.

"I'm not sure. I think I have couple of broken ribs, and I've been shot. I'll live if we can get the hell out of here."

They turned onto the winding road. Caleb looked back. Trees and darkness obscured the entrance to the McCoy house, as if it had never existed at all.

Caleb glanced over at Pete. He was leaning forward, trying to concentrate on the road.

Caleb could feel Sara shivering.

"Millstone shot her too, Pete. She's not doing so good."

Pete reached over and stroked her neck, then patted her on the head.

"Well, I know a good vet; actually, he's the only vet I know. I'll call him when we get you to my house."

"Pete, aren't you scared? Why are you putting yourself out for me like this? I don't know if you understand how crazy these people are. They're killers."

Pete did not hesitate.

"Because you need help. I don't know...I haven't been livin' much since my wife passed on. I feel like I haven't been of much use, as least til now. It feels pretty good. Do you know what I mean?"

Caleb certainly did. Even though he was battered and afraid, he felt a newfound power flowing through him, tickling the roof of his mouth. It was a terrible adventure, but an adventure nonetheless. For the first time in his life, he was taking part in life; feeling, giving and weaving himself into it so that his every word and action would later be the subject of scrutiny, affecting the course of events for many years to come.

"We're almost in town," Pete announced.

Caleb gawked at him in disbelief.

"Isn't there another way, Pete? They're going to be waiting for us!"

"That's the only road in or out of here, and you sure can't walk through the woods."

"Oh shit," Caleb whispered to himself as the soft outline of buildings came into view.

The truck sputtered and lurched slowly along the quiet streets. An occasional street lamp cast an eerie yellow light, providing a glimpse of quiet houses and yards and corners, none of which gave any hint of a human presence. Caleb was thankful for the strange stillness because it made him wonder whether anyone cared at all if he slipped away into Pennsylvania, into the annals of their cocktail party lore. He imagined that they forgot to set their alarms so they simply slept all night and cursed themselves in the morning when they found out that he had escaped.

But as they reached the last block before the end of town, where the road disappeared into the forest once again, they were waiting for him. Perhaps a dozen pairs of headlights were blazing, forming a wall of blinding light. Pete stopped the truck, then moved it forward once more. Caleb reached over and grabbed his arm.

"Don't bother, Pete."

"Maybe we can shake 'em back in town, maybe we can circle around again and get through."

"No, there's no point. We're just delaying the inevitable now. I'm going to get out. I'm going to try to talk to them. They probably haven't seen us yet. Take Sara and try heading the other way. They only want me, they won't be looking for you. It's the only way. There's no use in both of us getting stopped. Besides, you have got to find Kim, I don't want his blood on my hands either."

Caleb closed his eyes and shook his head. "This is pure insanity, a world gone completely mad. The only thing I can do is try to talk some sense into them. There's nowhere to run."

Pete shrugged his shoulders and sighed.

"All right," he whispered. "What do you want me to do?"

"When you get across the river into Pennsylvania, go right to the state police. I don't care what you tell them, just get them over here. Tell them there's a riot or something. Better yet, tell them another cop got shot, they should come running. Get Sara to a vet too, as soon as possible."

He set Sara down on the seat and opened the door. He waited behind a tree until Pete's truck disappeared in the darkness behind him. Caleb stepped out into the street. He shaded his eyes against the lights, but he could not distinguish any figures behind the glare. He stumbled forward toward the confrontation.

"That's far enough," a man's nervous voice demanded.

Caleb stopped. He was swaying back and forth, concentrating all his will to keep from falling over. Once again, the fear made him lash out with venomous fury.

"Your sheriff is dead, so is Maximillian McCoy. Are you people ready to take their places? Are you ready to kill me right now just to keep people from knowing about all of this?"

Their self-appointed leader stepped forward and met Caleb in the street. He was short and balding, probably in his forties. He wore glasses that kept slipping down his nose so that he was constantly pushing them back. He was wearing slacks, a dress shirt and a tailored sport coat. He kept glancing over his shoulder back toward the headlights.

"I'm...I'm sorry but we can't let you go," he said as if he were apologizing for bumping into him on a busy sidewalk. "We could be arrested, everything taken away."

"Look at me!" Caleb screamed. "Are you people out of your fucking minds? People are dead because of this place, because of you and your fucking forefathers. Don't you understand that it's over, finished! Maybe there's no way out for me, but the same goes for you. If not me, it'll be someone else, you still have to face reality!"

The bald man stepped back and raised his hands as if to protect himself.

"You have to understand too," he pleaded, trying to convince himself more than Caleb, "everything we are is tied up in our past. Without that we have nothing."

"Do you know how many people have died just to keep you comfortable? Do you know that Millstone killed anyone who tried to leave here, just to keep you in your BMW? Does it even make any difference at all that other people had their heads smashed and their brains blown out, all in the name of this cruddy, stuck-up shit town?"

"We had nothing to do with Millstone, we didn't know he hurt anybody."

"Maybe, maybe not, but you turned a blind eye to him, giving him permission to do whatever had to be done. Are you prepared now to shed my blood, are your ready to get your hands dirty?"

Enraged and brimming with confidence gained from their startled hesitation, Caleb walked past the bald man to the cars. "Why are you people hiding back here? Why don't you come out and meet the man you're going to kill? Come out here and get to know me."

Suddenly, another man appeared in front of Caleb, a baseball bat drawn back, ready to strike. Caleb closed his eyes and waited for sweet nothingness. But the only sensation he felt was his own labored breath and the searing pain in his side.

The man looked younger than the others, perhaps in his late thirties, and was only a little taller than Caleb. He was shaking and sneering with anger, but still he did not swing. He looked like any man who might have a family, a home. He was any person Caleb could have passed on the street and nodded to under different circumstances.

Caleb screamed so close to his face that he could smell his sweat.

"What the fuck are you waiting for? Go ahead, finish me off!"

Shocked, the man stepped back and lowered the bat.

"You coward," a woman's voice rang out, "you sniveling coward. I might have known for all your talk that you would do nothing."

Caleb followed the sound of her voice.

She was leaning against a Mercedes with her arms crossed. It was the blonde, well-dressed woman he had seen with her children in town when he first arrived.

"Why is he a coward, because he won't kill me?"

She rolled her eyes and looked away.

"You are nothing, not even an animal. You and the rest of the world. You live like pigs, stacked on top of each other in your cities. Then you have the nerve to come out here to our town, our paradise, and tell us how we should live. My family came over on the Mayflower. I won't even look at you, you half-breed, you don't even deserve to be acknowledged."

"Shut up Karen!" the younger man screamed. "What the hell do you know about anything? You can't even kill a spider, you run screaming from the room."

The man dropped the bat onto the ground. He shook his finger at the woman.

"No, I'm not going to do anything. I'm going home. If you want to do something you're going to have to do it yourself."

Caleb took a step forward, and the rest of the figures stepped back. Some of them whispered to each other. He turned and started to walk down the street past the group.

"One foot in front of the other," he whispered to himself.

"Are we just going to let him walk away?" another in the group asked.

"What the hell are we supposed to do?" a different voice responded.

Caleb reached out his hands, he could almost touch his freedom, even taste it on the moist night air. He laughed to himself. He had bluffed death, and death had failed to call him on it. Suddenly, his pain seemed to fade. With each step he grew stronger, lighter on his feet, supremely certain that he would soon be home, and Trinity would be at his side. There was nothing that could stop them. He laughed out loud now, and he did not care if anyone heard him. He laughed so loud that he did not hear the footsteps behind him.

He heard the bat hit the back of his head, though. There was a moment before he hit the ground when everything around him, even his own thoughts, moved in super slow motion. He saw the ground rushing up at him, frame-by-frame, inch-by-inch. He saw his hands move out in front of him to break the fall. He felt the shock wave of the blow radiate throughout his body, passing through synapse after synapse.

But the blow had not been strong enough to knock him unconscious. He rolled over and found the woman standing over him, the bat raised awkwardly over one shoulder. Her face was ghastly, contorted with a madness that she focused on him. She swung again, this time hitting Caleb squarely in the chest. He groaned and choked for breath. The woman raised the bat yet again. Behind her, Caleb could see others were coming.

Just as the woman swung the bat down, Caleb kicked at her kneecap with all his strength. He heard the sharp crackle of bone and sinew when the joint buckled backward. She fell, screaming. But no sooner had she toppled, than the others attacked.

Caleb curled up to protect himself against the vicious beating. Several blows, then more in rapid succession. Their twisted, drooling faces circled above him, gripped by a bloodlust no man should ever witness. They kicked and punched him, letting loose their own self-hatred. He felt himself slipping away. But just when he thought he saw the dark blue skies of forever, the blows began to subside. Caleb raised his head only to find another struggle underway.

A man in flowing, soft robes was moving quickly among the crowd. With lighting quick, almost effortless movements, the man struck and incapacitated each attacker. They barely had time to behold the strange man before he was there, toe to toe, striking them down. Most did not even manage to raise a hand before they fell. If they did, the figure ducked, or brushed it aside, came in close, struck a blow to the chest or neck, and another body was on the pavement. Caleb blinked his eyes several times in rapid succession to be sure he was not once more in the foggy world of semi-conciousness. No, he decided, he was not dreaming. All around him they were on their backs writhing in silent agony, or on their knees, trying to take in the precious breath that had been stolen by the stranger.

Someone gripped Caleb firmly and pulled his dead weight from the street. Caleb knew the kind, broad smile. He coughed several times and found blood in his hand.

"Kim?"

"Mr. Magellan. I apologize for these events, but I found the violence that I perpetuated necessary to spare you further injury."

Caleb reached out and rested a hand on Kim's shoulder.

Between breaths he explained what was happening, why they both had to leave immediately. Calmly, Kim listened. Those on the ground began to stir and take their feet. But they did not attack again. Wary, they stumbled back on their heels, still dazed by the foggy vision of a deadly, demon monk. But in the distance, more headlights, more angry silhouettes. They charged down the street at them.

Caleb shot Kim a wide-eyed, panicked glance.

"We won't make it, Kim, there's too many now."

Kim examined the crowd moving toward them.

"We cannot defeat so many, you are correct. But certainly I can block their path, slow them while you make an escape."

Caleb hesitated. His body begged for flight, but his mind resolved to stand with Kim, to satisfy his honor and dignity. After all, how far could he really get in a place where he didn't even know where he was going? He was prepared to go down swinging if necessary. But it wasn't Kim's fight.

"Why don't you go Kim? You want to die for me?"

Kim smiled. "It is not just for you that I would fight, but for all the souls trapped in this place. I sense them, waiting to be released. This cannot occur until their tragic deaths are revealed, and you are the only one who really knows. You are the only one who can prove the dead ever existed at all. It is my duty to assist you in such a time of need. I can do this best by making sure you escape. It would be futile for both of us to be cut down in this street."

The pack was almost on them. Caleb started to run. He looked back once last time. Kim bowed, then readied himself. He raised his hands in front of him, then stepped back with his right foot.

Caleb sprinted towards the darkness and the river where he might lose himself in the night. He turned a corner, slipped and fell. He smacked the pavement. By the time he clambered unsteadily to his feet again, two figures were right behind him. He stumbled across the street. Everything was blurry and swirling, miles away. He felt his way along the side of a building. Voices and heavy breathing behind him grew closer and closer. Caleb crawled underneath a fence and through some bushes. Thorns scratched his face, his skin felt like it was on fire. A hand grabbed his ankle, then slipped away. Somehow, he limped across a lawn. When the ground dropped away, he found himself suspended in mid-air for a moment, flying through the night. He glimpsed the perfect moon, hovering, waiting for him. He grasped for it, seemingly close enough to touch its glowing beauty before he dove down into blackness.

Spinning, rolling head over heels, he tumbled down the bank. He crashed through branches, narrowly missing the trunk of a gnarled tree. His head bounced, his bones bent and vibrated from the impacts. His skin ripped in places when it snagged on sharp things. Then, in a cloud of sand and dust, he slammed into the whispering river.

The water filled his mouth and his nostrils. The cold shocked him, and he opened his eyes. Shiny bits of moonlight penetrated the murkiness. Caleb swam for his life.

Chapter 21

WHILE CALEB FLOUNDERED IN the current, it whisked him away on its breath. Occasionally, when he managed to gulp a mouthful of fresh air, he could see people running along with him, on top of the cliff. They tried to keep up, but trees and buildings blocked their way. A shot rang out, then another. The surface of the water exploded only a few feet away. Caleb ducked beneath the slippery waves, whirling and tumbling. He struggled to keep his feet pointed down river, to protect his head and soften any collisions with the boulders that sometimes funneled the water through narrow channels at breakneck speed.

Suddenly, the water was once more smooth and gentle, massaging his wounds, it seemed, with a million fingers that held him up so he could breath. Caleb looked up. The stars and moon had followed him too, as if they were as fixated upon him as he was upon their light and power. He wondered if they mocked him, or loved him, rooted for him or cheered for more blood.

Caleb drifted around a small island with trees leaning to and fro, beneath a canopy of leaves that shut out the sky. His feet touched something hard. He felt along the object's length. It was a car, overturned.

Its wheels were just beneath the surface of the water. He grabbed the door latch. He needed a flashlight, a gun, anything that could serve as a weapon or tool to give him an advantage.

Caleb turned the handle. Something came out, rushed at him in the black water. A bloated face, vaguely familiar, skin bursting with white, shark-like eyes, stared at him. Arms slipped around Caleb, dragging him down to the muddy bottom. Caleb glimpsed a gold watch flickering in the swirling dirt. Frazier McCoy had come back from the dead.

Caleb panicked. He punched and kicked at the body, fighting the limp, dead weight. He was drowning. His lungs burned and ached, fighting to gasp, even if it meant sucking in the muddy water. Finally, Caleb untangled himself and broke through the surface. Using a sort of limping sidestroke, he fought through the current to the shore of the tiny island.

He made his way through the trees to the center, where he was completely hidden. In a tiny clearing, he found rings of stones blackened by fires. Empty beer bottles were strewn about, discarded by campers, teenagers no doubt.

In the distance, on the road above the riverbank, he could see headlights. Some sped by, but others stopped. Flashlights searched the water for him. Caleb ducked down as they swung over the island, scanning for movement, any sign of life.

When they had apparently given up looking for him, Caleb explored his surroundings. The island was about one quarter of a mile around, covered mostly by tall, thin trees that had somehow taken root in the sandy soil. On one end, he found the remains of an old cabin, its walls and roof long rotted away, leaving only an outline of its foundation in the dirt and a rusted cast iron stove.

A cold wind curled over the island. Caleb began to shiver and shake. He had nothing to keep him warm, nothing to use to start a fire. He searched through the debris of the cabin and found an iron bar. Caleb discovered he could wade out to Frazier's car, the water just covering his chest. Using the piece of metal, he forced open the trunk lid. Caleb reached inside and felt a small piece of hard-sided luggage and a square plastic container about the size of a shoebox. He brought them back to the shore, then dragged them to the old cabin.

Frazier's clothes were still dry. Caleb stripped off his wet clothing and pulled on a pair of Frazier's khaki shorts and a dark sweatshirt. They were at least three sizes too large. The small plastic box was a roadside emergency kit. Inside, Caleb found a first aid kit, several flares and some tools, all still dry.

Caleb started a fire inside the old woodstove with one of the flares, then quickly forced the door shut. He knew it might alert those searching for him, but, with the pain and cold seeping into his bones, he was willing to roll the dice. He curled up next to the small fire, but he could not sleep. Every noise was suspicious, ominous. Even the whisper of the rushing water was something to fear because it could easily disguise their approach. He strained his ears to distinguish the water's voice from other innocuous sounds of the night, always ready to run if he had to.

In the first morning light, Caleb placed a stick between his teeth and bit down hard to quell his screams while he swathed his wounds with antibacterial ointment. He also had a burning thirst. It drove him to crawl to the water in spite of his overwhelming fatigue. He did not care about the mud and muck dissolved in it, but only about swallowing as much of the brown stuff as his stomach could hold.

Caleb found shade and safety in some thick underbrush beneath a tree. From his position, he could see across the water to Pennsylvania. There was no break in the thick green cover of forest as far as he could see. Caleb decided that when it was dark again, he would float down the river. He knew it flowed south, toward the sea, toward the safe haven of civilization.

This time, Caleb slept as if in a coma. After what only seemed to be a mere flutter of his eyelids, he woke up to darkness once more. When he tried to move, his body did not immediately respond. Slowly, painfully, his cramped muscles finally cracked and gave in to his commands. First he sat up. Then, after he caught his breath, he gingerly stood up, using a tree for support. The moon was once more full and glowing. Although it would be easy for Caleb to find his way in the white light, it would also be easy for anyone to see him bobbing in the water.

Caleb placed his sweatshirt, the flashlight and the flares back in the plastic box, and put that box in the suitcase. He slid into the cold water and clung to the suitcase, using it to help him float. He kicked his feet until he was in the middle of the river where the current was swiftest.

He could only pray that Trinity had already found a way out.

Chapter 22

TRINITY WAITED BENEATH THE trees for the last of them. She glanced across the rusting bridge where the old railroad bed disappeared into the forest on the other side of the river, into Pennsylvania. For almost twenty four hours, without any sleep, she had ushered them, encouraged them, even cursed at them to get them to cross over. Some of them stayed though, preferring the security of their prison to the unknown. And now, her work was almost finished.

Trinity slid a small backpack off her shoulders. She pulled out one of her magazines. She did not even have to see the page to find it. Trinity knew every page, every crease, every wrinkle by heart. Although the picture was already carved permanently into her mind, she could not help looking at it once more in the moonlight.

It was a white, windswept beach. The sun was setting behind a pink sky. Ocean waves rolled in, churning softly on the sand. A couple in the distance walked hand in hand. Underneath the photograph it read "The Florida Keys. The keys to unlocking your soul." Trinity sighed. It was the first place she would go when she was safe, when she could be like everybody else.

Something moved. Trinity put the magazine back in her pack.

"C'mon," she whispered while she motioned wildly with both hands for the women to hurry up. "You're it, let's go!"

Trinity sat down and wiped the sweat from her forehead with the back of her sleeve. She felt her leg. The stump was numb and bloodied, ripe for an infection, she knew. Her mother sat down beside her. She stared at Trinity curiously, almost in awe. No doubt she wondered where Trinity found the strength to lead the others. Her mother stroked her hair.

"Go on mom, I'll be right behind you."

"Your father was tough like you, that's where you got it from."

Trinity smiled. She hugged her mother, then watched her cross the bridge, her figure silhouetted in the moonlight for a fleeting moment, finally melting into the darkness on the other side. Trinity followed her. Halfway across the bridge, Trinity stopped, ensnared by the lure of the white-hot moon that guided her to freedom.

She looked back from where she came, then to where she was going. But for a moment, she stood there on the bridge, between the two poles, between the known and unknown, between death and life. She raised her arms to the sky and closed her eyes. She breathed in and out, felt her heart pumping, her chest heaving and falling, her brain energized. For the first time, she knew what it meant to be alive. For the first time, she could feel God standing by her side.

A noise, maybe a gasp, came from somewhere in the dark. Trinity pressed herself against one of the steel beams and held her breath. She heard it again, a faint choking sound.

"Momma," she whispered. "Momma, are you there, are you okay?"

Her mother suddenly appeared, her face emerging from the darkness. She moaned, then gasped for air. Her eyes grew wide, then bulging.

"Momma?"

Millstone loosened the wire around her mother's neck and dropped her body. It fell to the bridge like a sack of cement. Her head hit one of the rails with a muffled crack.

Sheriff Millstone stepped out into the moonlight.

Trinity fell to her knees. It was only a ghost, a figment of her imagination. She had killed him, watched his body twitch and jerk. Still, there he was, moving closer to her. Trinity could plainly see the white bandage wrapped around his head, even beneath his wide hat. He paused for a moment to carefully wipe her mother's blood from his hands with a handkerchief he pulled from his shirt pocket.

"Well missy, I bet you thought you were pretty clever. You sneak up behind me and hit me on the head, then you're rid of the big bad wolf, right?"

Millstone kneeled down next to her and smiled. For a long moment he searched her eyes, enjoying the terror he saw there.

"I have to tell you though, you hit pretty hard for a girl. Besides the concussion and the bad headache, the doc' had to put ten stitches in the back of my head. I guess I need to have eyes back there whenever you're around, huh?"

Trinity was sobbing. Millstone gently touched her neck, then lifted up her chin.

"Don't worry, you little bitch. I won't kill you, at least until I find that friend of yours."

Millstone ran his fingers along the length of her thigh.

"But that doesn't mean we can't have some fun in the meantime. You look pretty sweet, at least from the waist up, at least for a cripple."

He grabbed Trinity by the throat and began to squeeze.

"So where is he, where is that fuckin' troublemaker?"

Trinity shook her head.

"Not good enough." He clenched his teeth and squeezed harder. "I need to know exactly where he is."

Trinity shook her head once more.

"He's already gone," Trinity managed to gurgle.

Millstone released his grip and Trinity fell forward, choking and coughing.

Millstone stood up and glanced around.

"Somehow, I don't think he'd leave without you. Or if he did, he'd come back lookin' for you."

Millstone grabbed Trinity by her hair and dragged her to her feet. He slammed her against one of the iron beams, then produced a length of rope and tied her hands behind her around the beam. He pulled the knot so tight that her fingers instantly went numb.

"I'm gonna' keep you here for a while, while I have a look around."

As Millstone passed Trinity's mother, he picked the body up and threw it over the side of the bridge almost effortlessly.

Trinity started to scream.

"Go ahead and scream, you little bitch. In case you thought your friends might help, I just thought you should know that they're down there in the water with your momma."

Trinity spit, grunted and struggled against the rope. She kicked her legs into the air, but her blows fell far short of her target. Millstone only laughed, then took his off his hat. He began to unbuckle his holster belt.

"I'll give you something to scream about, you little bitch."

Trinity closed her eyes. She wanted to fight him to the last, wanted to kick him and tear off his flesh with her teeth, but she was exhausted. The child in her mind whisked her away to safety, to hide her from the tragedy. Maybe it was someplace she had been, or perhaps only read about in one of her magazines. She was sitting alone on a sun-baked, pebbly shore. Waves were lapping gently at her feet, tickling her toes. Her body was not bruised or battered, but tan and soft, including both of her long, smooth legs.

Chapter 23

THE OLD BRIDGE WAS illuminated almost as brightly by the moon as it had been in the afternoon light the day Caleb had gone fishing with Pete. The store was dark though, silent. Caleb could only hope Pete had made it out safely. He doubted Mr. Kim had escaped. Caleb's eyes welled with tears. He shook his head and gritted his teeth. This was no time for tears.

The gangly structure was a welcome sight, something hard and real, a sign showing him the way to safety and people. Where there was a bridge spanning water, there was a path on the other side. Where there was a path, there was a destination worth finding.

Caleb quietly paddled to the shore, just beneath the towering skeleton of metal. He dragged himself out of the water and lay silent. He could hear little over the cicadas and the rushing water, but he could see nobody moving. He searched around for a moment and quickly found the ghost outline of a trail leading up a steep slope to the bridge above. Slowly, Caleb crawled and pulled himself over the rocks. His ribs began to throb and burn again, making it feel as if each time he brushed against the ground, his bones were breaking all over again. He stopped every so often just to catch his breath.

When Caleb reached the top, he crouched down, once more alert for any movement. He started across the bridge. When he saw them, he dropped down and lay flat on the railroad ties beneath the tracks. Trinity was tied to a piece of the superstructure, limp and slumped forward. Millstone was staring out into the darkness.

It isn't possible, he thought, *the man is dead and gone, stinking and rotting away by now.*

Millstone suddenly whirled around in Caleb's direction. Caleb dropped his head and stared down into the empty space below. A pebble fell, glowed in the moonlight for a moment, and then disappeared. He could not help but think of himself as so small and powerless.

Caleb began to hyperventilate. He closed his eyes for a moment, trying to control his breathing. He looked up again, and Millstone was gone. He swiveled his head in all directions, but there was no sign of him. Caleb rubbed his eyes. Maybe it was nothing at all, just a fear played out in the shadows and the light. But Trinity was still there, hanging and lifeless.

Caleb crawled over to her and knelt down. He lifted her chin.

"Trinity, it's me, Caleb."

There was no response.

Caleb pulled her hair back out of her eyes. Gently, he smacked one of her cheeks.

"Trinity!" he screamed as loud as a whisper would allow, "Trinity!"

Her eyelids shuddered then opened, glassy slits. She smiled.

"Trinity, what happened, are you all right? Where's Millstone?"

"I don't know," she said with a soft but far-away look on her face, as if she had just been plucked from heaven.

"Are you all right?"

"I don't know," she whispered again. "I'm just tired, so tired. Can't you let me sleep awhile?"

Caleb untied her and laid her down on the bridge. He could see her clothes had been torn and ripped away. Blood dripped down the inside of her legs in dark lines.

"Did he do this to you, did Millstone do this to you?"

Trinity reached up and touched his lips with her finger as if to hush him, then closed her eyes once more. Caleb watched her take several breaths, each one more shallow than the last. Then she was gone. About that time, he heard the footsteps behind him.

Millstone's shadow, complete with uniform hat, cast long across the bridge ahead of Caleb. Caleb turned and lunged at him, prepared to kill them both because he had nothing else to lose. Before Millstone could draw his pistol, Caleb wrapped his arms around him and pushed and pumped his legs with all his might, flinging them both off the bridge, spiraling down into the night. Caleb held on to him when they hit the water and sank to the bottom. Caleb held Millstone even tighter while he squirmed and screamed and finally choked on the mud. Caleb continued to squeeze and pull Millstone down into the slimy ooze until he was sure that every void and crevice in Millstone's body was filled with black water.

Caleb tried to reach the surface, but could not hold his breath any longer. Just when he could see a light from above the waves, he opened his mouth and the river rushed in. He closed his eyes and let himself fall back down into the depths. But, strangely enough, the light grew brighter, more intense. Perhaps he had found heaven, or perhaps it was the hot flames of hell, where his father was waiting for him.

Chapter 24

CALEB PERCHED HIMSELF ON top of the picnic table outside his cabin just as the sun fell behind the bare, red rock. He glanced around, as if to assure himself that he had not suddenly been transported back in time, back to the dense, moist forest, back to the house of McCoy. But there was no mistaking Utah's hot, barren moonscape. It was more like Mars really, glowing blood red in the last of day's light.

Caleb leaned back on his elbows, but had to sit back up when he felt a sharp pain working its way down his shoulder. He rotated his arm in the socket several times until the sensation faded.

"Six months now and it still isn't right," he whispered.

Caleb stared at Sara sleeping inside the doorway of the cabin, curled up in a ball.

He whistled.

Sara got up and shook herself violently, then pranced over to Caleb and sat on the ground. Sara had suffered more than him, Caleb thought. But he was amazed at how well she had adapted to moving on only three legs. She was as fast as she had ever been, perhaps even stronger now. Caleb pulled a small dog biscuit from one of his pockets and threw it high into the air. Sara leaped several feet off the ground, using her single hind leg for propulsion, and snatched the biscuit in one fluid motion. Caleb patted her on the head while she chewed.

One month ago, Caleb quit his job, packed what he could in the Stingray and a small trailer and headed west. His mother said he could stay with her until his head was clear. He stopped in beautiful places he found along the way. He drove and slept under the stars and wondered mostly about Trinity, Kim and the other lives lost.

In the beginning of his journey he only napped fitfully, tortured by dreams and a guilty conscience. Even though he could sleep through most of the night now, Caleb still cursed himself for not saving her. Trinity still often appeared in his dreams. But she was always smiling, softly, innocently, as if she were looking down on him from the stars that burned like flash bulbs in the big western sky. He got the feeling that she had forgiven him. He missed her so desperately sometimes that he wondered why he shouldn't follow her by his own hand. But a strange feeling of sharp purpose always found him at those moments. He knew he had other things to do before he died; he simply had no clue what they were.

Caleb's cell phone started to chime. He sighed and rubbed his eyes.

The world had certainly not forgotten about him. He hoped it was Pete. He had said he wanted to take a long vacation in Europe, and Caleb had offered to run the store for him while he was gone. Caleb felt a little guilty about that too. He wished he could give Pete something more. After all, it was Pete who had pulled him from the river and somehow brought him back to life. And it was Pete who had come to the hospital every day to see him.

Caleb glanced at the number of the caller. He did not recognize it. Caleb was fairly sure, though, that the call was from one of the many detectives and politicians who had interviewed him no less than two dozen times about what had happened in Promise.

For a while the District Attorney considered bringing charges against him for the deaths of Millstone, his deputy and Maximillian McCoy, but they quickly forgot about him when the scope of dark dealings in Promise was revealed. The last day he was in the hospital, Caleb received a letter from the District Attorney's office. They had decided not to prosecute him. They said their investigation revealed that his actions were "justified."

Caleb read in the New York Times that Congress was going to hold hearings to determine if reparations should be paid to the families of slaves who had died in Promise. The article reported that the FBI was using DNA taken from bone material to trace the families of the dead. Pete said they had been excavating the ground around the McCoy house day and night for weeks. He told Caleb that the government had put up so many lights around the property it looked like a football stadium.

Caleb took several deep breaths. The great expanse all around him beckoned him powerfully. The silence screamed for him to explore the night and the roads that led to its heart. As darkness fell, the air cooled rapidly. A good time to drive, he thought, out of the burning sun.

Sara slept on the seat next to him while they chewed up the endless highway. The Stingray roared through the night, stirring nocturnal animals. Crouched low to the ground, their glowing eyes flashed red for a moment then disappeared into the loose, dry brush.

Several times, Caleb pulled off to one of the many scenic overlooks that gave him a view of the canyons. He stood on the edge of the cliffs, looking out onto the fathomless miles of scarred limestone. The moonlight reflected strangely off the light rock, playing tricks with the dark. It was always Trinity's face he thought he saw there.

But Caleb's eyelids finally grew heavy, and he searched for a place to stop. He had a tent and a sleeping bag, and any place where he happened to bed down for the night was home.

As he passed a dirt road, he thought he noticed something. It was just a shape really, maybe a sign, somewhere along the side of the road as he passed. Caleb stopped the car and turned around. His headlights illuminated it. He gasped.

The sign read "Promise." Underneath an arrow pointed toward the narrow road that disappeared over the horizon.

CPSIA information can be obtained at www.ICGtesting.com
Printed in the USA
LVOW09s1733291014

411074LV00003B/633/P

9 781412 061032